A Tempting Proposal

Dara Girard

A Tempting Proposal

ISBN13:978-1949764109

Printed in the United States of America
Cover photo © 2017 Heather Moreau /123rf
Cover and Layout Copyright © 2017 Ilori Press Books, LLC

This is a work of fiction. Names, characters, places, and incidents either are the product of the author's imagination or are used fictitiously, and any resemblance to actual persons, living or dead, business establishments, events or locales is entirely coincidental.

ILORI PRESS BOOKS, LLC
P.O. Box 10332
Silver Spring, MD 20914

www.iloripressbooks.com

To my wonderful readers!

Other books by Dara Girard

The Black Stockings Society

Power Play

A Gentleman's Offer

Body Chemistry

Round the Clock

Return of the Black Stockings Society

Playing for Keeps

After Hours

A Private Affair

Just One Look

Private Lessons

Henson Series

Table for Two

Gaining Interest

Careless Rapture

Dangerous Curves

Familiar Stranger

The Clifton Sisters

The Sapphire Pendant

The Amber Stone

It Happened One Wedding
Unexpected Pleasure
Midnight Promise
Sweet Temptation
Always and Forever

Novels
Illusive Flame
Honest Betrayal
The Daughters of Winston Barnett
Remember My Name

Chapter One

A wife.

He was not supposed to end up with a wife. At least not yet. He had plans, dreams and goals. This was not one of them. James Fortune gritted his teeth as he listened to the melodious soft voice of Pastor Valentine, her pink reading glasses hanging precariously low on her nose, inches away from falling. Much like the present state of his life.

He'd managed to achieve most of his goals. He'd gotten degrees in both Biology and Mechanical Engineering and become head of Research and Development at BioMed Solutions. Yes, it was his stepfather's company, and at thirty-four he was the youngest division manager in the company, but no one could deny that under James's watch and careful leadership more innovative projects had been developed and funded. Morale was up and the people liked him, unlike his predecessor, a charismatic man who wasted money on pet projects that only highlighted his interests instead of others or furthering the success of the company.

James knew he wouldn't stay in management for long, he wanted to launch his own ventures, but he'd given himself two more years before he would embark on his next career goal. He believed in taking calculated risks.

Not insane ones.

James glanced at Pastor Valentine's reading glasses again, noticing that they'd fallen down a little further. He flexed his fingers resisting the urge to say something. Couldn't she feel them moving? Would she let them fall off her face?

He inwardly groaned, knowing his attention and annoyance were misplaced. It wasn't the pastor's glasses that really bothered him, or even the sound of her voice, which always reminded him of someone in a musical about to burst into song (he half expected her to snap the bible shut, rip off her glasses and start singing), it was the entire ceremony.

He knew that what he was doing was not only reckless and insane, but criminal. He'd never done anything illegal in his life. Okay, so maybe he had done some speeding, and once—just once—when he was under charged for an item at the grocery store, he didn't report it. But he was a law abiding citizen. A good man. Now he was a fraud. He'd put his reputation and future on the line all because of Jackson.

His twin brother was supposed to be standing at the altar, inside this elegant stone cathedral, bearing the scrutiny of hundreds of guests from the Americas and the Caribbean, marrying the beautiful, brilliant and influential Ava Simone Hughes.

James made sure to keep his gaze on the pastor, instead of her. He knew Ava's brilliance by her reputation. She'd won an international science prize at sixteen and her research in the field of biodegradable implants preceded her. Her findings were almost legendary in the industry; her influence was also unavoidable from her innovative lab work to her connection with top universities. But her beauty.

That was his weak point.

He feared his heart would stop when the cathedral's double doors opened and she walked down the red carpeted, flower adorned aisle towards him. Damn, why did it have to be *him*? He'd always found her attractive, even in the dark suits she liked to wear—sometimes with trousers other times with a skirt, always black or dark blue—but at this moment she was breathtaking in a floor-length tulle lace gown with beaded sequins. The ivory colored fabric, accented with a translucent hint of sky blue, complimented her exquisite dark skin.

She looked like a princess, her carriage regal, her fine high cheekbones striking, but he knew she was no innocent, blushing bride. She had dangerous brown eyes and without the benefit of a veil to shield him from her gaze, he had to face them head on and make sure she didn't suspect a thing. She was the kind of woman who could kiss a man tenderly on the lips and drive a steak knife through his heart at the same time. He knew his deception would come at a price if she ever found out.

He couldn't let that happen. He had to be careful.

He'd discovered that the first time Jackson formerly introduced her to him. Her keen, steely gaze hit him like a brick. With one look he'd seen her power and vulnerability and that combination had floored him. He knew a woman like her could be trouble, but his brother liked courting trouble so James had dismissed the feeling. He couldn't dismiss it now.

James briefly looked at the ceiling. He was doing the right thing. Jilting a woman like Ava would have far reaching consequences and too much was at stake. He was doing this because his brother was too weak to accept his duty to his family and the business.

James took a deep breath, wishing he would wake up from this nightmare, but when he touched Ava's hand and slid a white gold band of hand selected diamonds on one of her long, slender fingers he knew it was all too real.

At least his hands didn't tremble and he didn't drop the ring as he feared, trying his best to ignore the reality that every action he made was being watched. Unlike his brother who welcomed it like a parched horse at a watering hole, he didn't like being in the spotlight. James inwardly groaned. He could use a drink right now. Something cold and biting. He stood stock still as he felt a trail of sweat slide down his back. He remembered saying "With this ring…" but the rest was a blur as he fought to imitate his brother's casual flair in every word and gesture.

He'd never switched places with Jackson before, despite all his brother's urgings when they were younger, trying to convince him that it would be fun. James never thought it would be either fun or practical. Definitely not practical. Even as a child he knew a day in the life of his brother would be exhausting.

Instead of being alone in the library, with his science club, discussing a new discovery with a teacher or training with the track team, he'd be charming the students (especially the girls, but guys liked him too) and teachers of both genders, and partying. There would be too many names to remember, too many places to be. He liked to live a regimented, quiet life and said he'd never switch places. Ever.

He'd been wrong.

But he didn't have a choice.

Chapter Two

James had sensed there was a problem last night at the rehearsal dinner when he'd found his brother in the dark tiled restaurant men's room. Jackson stood in front of one of the sinks, wiping water from his face with a paper towel.

"You've been gone nearly fifteen minutes," James said exasperated, looking at his brother in the mirror reflection. "What's wrong?" The dinner was a chance for the two families to get to know each other before the big event. James had been paired with Ava's Uncle, a boisterous man who liked to brag that the only exercise he did was work on his Molson muscle as he proudly patted his beer belly. Since he was the man giving Ava away tomorrow, she had told them she was not close to her father so he wouldn't be attending, James tried his best to laugh at all her uncle's jokes. But after his brother's disappearance he was starting to feel the strain of pretending.

Jackson threw away the paper towel then tugged on the collar of his purple shirt. "I can't do this."

"Do what?"

He stretched out his arms. "This. Everything. It's all a mistake."

"What are you talking about?"

Jackson looked at him with a flat expression. "You know what I'm talking about. I can't—"

James swore and shook his head. He usually knew what his brother was thinking, but this time he didn't want to believe it. He couldn't believe it. His brother's wedding mattered too much. "Shut up."

"Don't worry, no one else is in here."

James checked the stalls just to make sure before he looked at his brother again. "I don't care. Shut up and come back to the table."

"I have to say it."

James rested his hands on his hips and shook his head again. "No, you don't."

"I can't marry her. There's something about her. Something that's just not right. She scares me."

James playfully patted his brother on the side of his face and said with a grin, "She was always scary." He turned to the door. "Now come on."

"You noticed that too?"

James paused then slowly turned back to him. "It's hard to miss."

"It's those eyes, right? I didn't notice them before."

"She's not scarier than some of the other women you've been with."

Jackson waved his finger at him. "No, there's something different about her." He turned back to the mirror and gazed at his reflection. "I can't go through with it. I thought I could, but I was wrong."

James rested a hand on his brother's shoulder. "It's nerves. You're not scared of her, it's the thought of marriage that frightens you. You're worried about how marriage will change your life, and it will, for the better."

Jackson shook his head. "It's not that," he said in a grim tone. "There's just something I didn't notice before. I can't put my finger on it." He shifted his gaze to James's face. "You know I'm good at reading people when it's important."

James swept his hand past the faucet sensor, letting the hot water hit his palm and slide through his fingers. He cupped some water in his hand and threw it at his brother.

Jackson jumped back and scowled. "Watch the shirt."

James placed his wet palm on the dark marble counter. "Watch your mouth."

"I told you I had to say it," Jackson said, checking to see what possible damage the water had done to his shirt.

"It's arranged. It's planned."

Jackson smoothed down the front buttons of his shirt. "I know."

"Mom needs this."

Jackson looked up, met James's gaze and softly swore.

James nodded. He now had his brother's full attention and also had him where he wanted him—feeling guilty. Their mother was thrilled about the upcoming wedding and the chance to see one of her sons getting married. She had been like a little girl during the holidays taking care of all the preparations, which Ava had graciously allowed their mother to be a part of. James remembered when his mother had shyly hinted that since she'd had no daughters she'd been disappointed that she never would have the opportunity. When James had mentioned it to Ava, she'd expertly invited her to participate fully in all the wedding plans, he'd always be grateful for that.

Jackson sighed and nodded looking defeated. "You're right. You're right. Maybe it's just the thought of the ceremony. You know I hate things like that."

"No, you don't. You like being the center of attention."

"Just go along with me, okay?"

James grabbed a paper towel and dried his hands. "You'll be fine."

"What if I forget the words?"

"Just repeat what the pastor says."

Jackson nodded again and rubbed the back of his neck, looking just as miserable as he had before. "Right, right."

James patted him on the back. "You like her. She likes you. You work well together. A lot is riding on this and—"

Jackson tugged on his collar again. "I feel like I can't breathe." He sent a wary glance at the exit. "I can't go back in there. There's so much expectation from…"

"Edgar," James said when his brother didn't finish.

Their stepfather, Edgar Fortune, was founder of Bio-Med Solutions, a company that manufactured joint replacements, and with a growing aging population living longer with more active lives, business was booming. Edgar lived and breathed the business and loomed large in their lives. They both had vague memories of their father, an economics professor originally from Grenada, who'd disappeared a year after their younger brother Rudy was born.

Their mother had met Edgar through a mutual acquaintance at a cocktail party. Edgar swept into their lives when they were both six years old and captured their attention, if not their affection. He was a hard man to get close to. Jamaican born-US raised, in the state of Virginia, with a taste for Cuban cigars, boxing and fast horses. Driven, ruthless, with more women than most, many wondered why he'd decided to settle down with a woman with three children. A woman who, at the time, worked as a secretary for a speech pathologist. Almost thirty years later, people still wondered how the marriage had lasted.

Although Florence "Flo" Fortune had turned herself into the perfect corporate wife, her sweet manner was in direct contrast to her husband's. Soon after the marriage, Edgar adopted them and they lost their last name 'Brownson' and became Fortunes, and Edgar liked to constantly remind them of the same thing he'd told them the day of their adoption, "I gave you my name for a reason. It means your fortunes have changed. So you owe everything to me." And they believed him and worked hard to please him.

There was no fear, just expected loyalty and they were both eager to give it. When Edgar announced that it was time one of them got married it surprised everyone when Jackson said he'd met someone. They were even more surprised when he told them who she was—Ava Hughes. A woman whose small company had developed an injectable agent that could be used in various replacement joints. Most of the replacement joints their firm created had to be replaced over time due to erosion, slippage and/or growth, especially in children, but the agent Ava's company had developed was a biodegradable solution that allowed the joints to be able to stay in place longer and to eventually be replaced by the patient's own cells within two or three years.

Ava's arrival in their lives had come at an opportune time. Edgar had suffered a heart attack last year, making shareholders nervous. And there was the competition. While Ava's research and development was way ahead, attempts to steal and duplicate her success was a constant threat.

Edgar made it clear that it would be in Ava's best interest to join forces, both personally and professionally, offering her a handsome deal. It included a generous amount of shares; full access to the inner workings of the company; guaranteed bonus package and use of a state of the art research lab and funding to develop other ideas if she agreed to marry into the family. He didn't want any major position outside of his control. To James's surprise, Ava agreed to the deal and Jackson, in his carefree way, went along with it.

And now, eight weeks later, his brother was having second thoughts.

"Yes, I mean Edgar," Jackson said with a sigh. "What if I screw this up?"

"There's nothing to screw up."

"I just feel the pressure. It's happening too fast. I'm not good under pressure." He took off his jacket then unbuttoned his shirt.

James watched him in alarm. "What are you doing?"

"Just for tonight."

James shook his head, reading his brother's thoughts. He wanted to switch places. That wasn't going to happen. He held up his hands, warding him off. "Oh no." Although they were identical twins they both dressed very different and tonight was no exception.

"Just for a couple of hours."

James waved his hands. "No. Absolutely not."

Jackson took off his shirt. "Dinner's almost over anyway."

"No."

He held the shirt out to him. "Otherwise I'm walking out of here. I mean it," he added when James didn't move.

James swore. He knew his brother would. When he felt trapped, Jackson's first instinct was to run. "All right," James said, unbuttoning his own shirt, "but this is the first and last time I'll ever do this for you."

Jackson smiled. "Thanks."

James glared at him. "Save your thanks for later, I haven't pulled it off yet."

Chapter Three

The other one.

Ava knew the moment the vacant seat beside her was taken that its new occupant was 'the other one'. That's how she'd gotten used to thinking of James Fortune. While Jackson radiated light and energy, James radiated a more subtle heat.

She didn't know why he always made her feel too warm and uneasy. She never felt comfortable around him. She rarely felt comfortable around anyone, preferring the sight of a computer screen, microscopic organisms or a book to people, but he put her on edge in a way no one had before. He made her nervous. She couldn't understand why. She wasn't afraid, few things frightened her, and if she planned to marry into the Fortune family she'd have to be strong, but he still put her off-guard.

Jackson was easy to play with, fun, simple to read. She'd navigated their relationship by approaching Edgar first and getting into his good graces *before* she orchestrated her meeting with Jackson. She'd even made sure that Edgar thought the marriage arrangement had been his idea.

Such a strategy would be harder to pull off with James, but not impossible. He was just more…something she couldn't fathom and had no interest in figuring out. She had to marry Jackson for her plan to work. So she would wait and see what their next move would be.

As identical twins there was nothing about him that should have bothered her. He and Jackson shared the same tall, powerful physique reminiscent of the ancient Douglas fir tree she'd seen as a child growing up in Vancouver, British Columbia. She'd been amazed by their size and history and since then had been drawn to trees, hiding in them when she wanted to get away from her lonely days at home and school. James, however, would be no sanctuary. He was like a tree occupied by a black bear.

He and Jackson both had elegant, clean shaven features and even white teeth that contrasted with their smooth brown skin in an attractive way.

But that's where the similarities ended. In appearance they were identical, in personality and style they couldn't be more different. Jackson preferred loud, bold colors like the purple shirt he wore under his dark blue jacket with matching purple lapels, cotton slacks and shoes; James, in contrast, wore grey trousers matching his jacket and a simple white shirt. Of course now he didn't, since he was wearing his brother's clothes.

Ava had to tap down a wave of anger. What game were they playing? James had slipped into his brother's role well, returning to the table with a wide smile and making the guests laugh at a joke she'd heard Jackson make many times before, but she couldn't be fooled because James had given himself away. It was a small simple act no one else would easily notice, but it was something she'd used to distinguish them.

When James and Jackson had returned from the washroom to take a seat at the table, Ava watched as James noticed his younger brother. Their younger brother Randolph, who everyone called Rudy, had Down syndrome and although he had a mild form, earning a university degree and running his own business, he still had triggers that could upset him and James was fiercely protective.

That evening, Rudy had noticed his brothers' long absence from the table and that had upset him. Although his mother and stepfather tried to assure him, his mood grew more anxious and he wouldn't eat.

When they returned to the table that's when she saw it— Jackson took his seat (as James) without looking at anyone else, while James (as Jackson) quickly surveyed the mood of the table, saw Rudy's expression and paused. He took a moment and bent down next to his brother, said something that made his brother smile before he gently rubbed Rudy's cheek with his knuckles. It was a tender action she'd seen James do before and always seemed to have a calming affect on Rudy. His smile widened and James looked at his mother sending her a silent message before he took the seat next to Ava.

In those few seconds, he'd given himself away by doing something Jackson never did—comfort his brother and assuring his mother. Ava took a sip of her white wine, resisting the urge to dump it over his head and demand to know what he was up to. Were they trying to humiliate her? Did they think this upcoming wedding was a joke?

He nudged her with his elbow and said something that Jackson would say, in the cocky, funny way Jackson would say it. Ava didn't really pay attention because she knew it didn't matter. She did what was expected and smiled at him; he smiled in return. She held his gaze a lot longer than she should have but was unable, or unwilling, to look away, wondering if he could bear the full force of her gaze.

For a moment, a vulnerable hesitancy entered his brown gaze, and her grin widened a fraction in triumph. *You idiot. Your eyes aren't right. What are you trying to pull?*

Jackson's gaze was more carefree, more inviting, James's were too serious. He couldn't smile enough to take that sheen away.

But before she could bask in her small victory his eyes darkened with a glint of interest that made her grin fade as a wave of heat swept through her body. At first it felt faint then grew more intense. It was a feeling she never felt with Jackson and she wondered if his heated gaze reflected James's true interest or if it was part of the role he was playing.

If he thought this was how Jackson felt, he was doing it wrong, because Jackson never looked at her like that. He never made her feel as if he was marrying her for any other reason than to make his stepfather happy and for the company. Ava pulled her gaze away from his and silently seethed, hating her physical response to him. She'd wanted him to be the first to look away, but she'd get him back another way. She wouldn't let the Fortune brothers make a fool of her.

Chapter Four

"Is something the matter?" Flo asked her husband as she softly closed the door to their master bedroom. She was tired but happy after a long day and still full from the food she'd eaten at the rehearsal dinner.

She'd finished checking to make sure Rudy was safely tucked in bed and now found Edgar sitting on the side of their large platform bed with an unlit cigar in his hand. He usually did so when he was worried about something. Even in repose he looked ready to fight. He was a man of average height with a thick, muscular build, belying his advanced years, and skin the color of roasted almonds.

"Did Jackson seem different to you?" he asked in a low voice.

"Different how?"

He shrugged. "I don't know. At the wedding rehearsal he flubbed a few lines and at the rehearsal dinner… At first he seemed like he didn't want to be there and then he did."

"And why is that a problem?" Flo asked with a soft smile. "I think the reality of what he's doing is settling in."

Edgar's voice remained grim. "As long as that's all it is."

She sat down beside him but not close enough to touch. "He will not disappoint us."

Edgar sent her a dismissive glance before looking away. "You sound certain."

"I am. There will be a wedding tomorrow. I know my boys."

She tenderly touched his hand and he felt a moment of guilt, remembering the real reason why he'd married her. It wasn't for her soft, pretty features that age had been kind to, or her pleasing manner, which still gave him comfort in a way that surprised him. Few people could ease his bad mood the way she could.

At times he wondered if he'd made up for the selfish reason he'd asked her to be his wife. He'd had so much to prove and gain back then and now, so much to lose. That was the problem with years, intangible things like respect, dignity, and ones reputation, mattered more.

He'd raised his stepsons by instilling a tradition of loyalty that he never had. His father had been a useless plumber who'd managed to sleep with half of the housewives in the neighborhood, and rumored to have knocked up two before he was killed in a hit-and-run on his way home from a church bible study. But his father had left him with a love of boxing, which he'd instilled in him after starting him in the sport at the age of five, and a hunger to be somebody, because his father showed him that being a nobody was for punks.

His mother's brother, Uncle Frank, a barrel-chested man with an ability to inhale a cigarette and turn it into ash within minutes, had taken pity on them and given them a place to stay, begrudgingly, reminding them every moment he could that Edgar and his sister, and their father, had ruined their mother's life. How she'd been the smartest in the family and would have been the first to graduate from college if their father hadn't entered her life and sweet talked her into running off with him.

While he berated their very existence he also used them to his benefit, catching the eye of a wealthy woman at church who thought his care for his widowed sister and her children meant that he was a good man. He milked her sympathy into marriage, moving their entire family into her house, where he managed to work as little as possible, pretending he was helping his sister doing charity work while he lived off his wife's sense of obligation and Christian duty until she died.

From his uncle he learned the power of appearance and promised himself that he wouldn't be anybody's burden.

Edgar worked to prove his uncle wrong. He wasn't his father. He wasn't like any of them. He got his degree, in a field of study his uncle couldn't understand, bought his mother a house and even paid for his uncle's care until his death. Not that the bastard ever thanked him for it. He learned, on his own, what being a man was. What it took to survive in this world and gain respect.

And he'd passed that knowledge down. Now, more than ever, he needed to see it come to fruition. BioMed

Solutions, despite their global market and consistent business, had nearly run out of money twice due to overexpansion and costly, futile research that went nowhere. With Jackson's help he had been able to restructure the company and James had tightened the spending in R&D and their profits had grown again. He'd made a good investment in them.

He'd seen their potential early but never thought they would be this useful to him. Now the next piece was taking BioMed Solutions to the next level. Ava Hughes's new product could take them beyond their competitors in a way that would last for generations. He needed this wedding to go without a hitch. He stared at the ground, thinking of his uncle. He wanted to achieve a level of success that would continue to make the old bastard turn in his grave.

Chapter Five

This was not what he'd expected.

James ran a hand down his face, wondering how he'd ended up in Ava's apartment. No, he knew how he'd gotten there he just couldn't believe he hadn't managed to come up with an excuse to get out of it. He'd played Jackson long enough and now had entered dangerous territory.

He closed his eyes and reimagined the scene in the men's room in the restaurant. He should have taken Jackson's shirt and thrown it back at him. He should have forced him to get through the evening and said they'd talk about it later. Maybe he should have bribed him. His brother loved classic cars. He could have said he'd buy him one. Instead, he'd listen to him and now he was sitting on a couch that felt as comfortable as a cement block. Or maybe that was just how he was feeling, he couldn't seem to get comfortable.

He pounded his fist on the cushion and swore when pain shot through his hand. No, it was the couch. It was hard as stone. He lifted the fitted sofa cover to see what it was made out of and paused when he saw stacks of hardcover books—some textbooks, some coffee table books. What the heck?

James crouched down and lifted the cover higher just to make sure. They were books alright, but were they real? He poked a spine with his forefinger surprised when it shifted. They were actually real books not fakes fused together. Who makes furniture out of books? Did his brother know about this?

"Do you want anything to eat?" Ava called out to him from the kitchen where the smell of coffee was filling the air.

James gently tried to put the book back in place, but failed. "No, I'm fine." He let the sofa cover fall and sat back on the couch, wincing when he sat down too hard. At least he knew one thing; Ava didn't expect him to get comfortable.

Ava hummed with malicious pleasure as she prepared coffee. She knew James was sweating in the other room and she planned to enjoy every second of it. She'd almost laughed at the expression of shock on his face when she'd told him to drive her home after dinner had ended and people started to leave.

"I said I would what?" he said, while helping her put on her coat.

"Drive me home." She smiled up at him over her shoulder. "Don't you remember?"

"Yes, of course." He looked towards Jackson who was talking to Flo. "Let me just—"

Ava looped her arm through his, trapping him. She wouldn't let him get away and switch places again. She'd make him pay a little for his deception. "They'll be fine."

"I know but—"

She led him towards the exit before he could catch his brother's attention. "We've already said our goodbyes."

"But Rudy—"

"Is with James. It's not like you to worry. You know that James takes care of everything."

His jaw twitched. She hid a grin knowing she'd struck a nerve. He nodded and held the door open for her. "Right."

She paused. "You don't sound happy. I thought you looked forward to spending some time alone with me."

He nodded again, his expression briefly becoming more resolute before it softened into a smile. "I did—uh do." He winked. "I was just building up for tomorrow night."

She returned his smile then walked past him and let it fall as she headed out into the parking lot. The warm spring evening breeze brushed her skin and the scent of roses from the bushes lining the restaurant greeted her. She would have enjoyed the aroma if she hadn't been annoyed. Her heels clicked along the gravel path, her black skirt whispering against her legs. It took her a moment to realize hers was the only footsteps she heard. Had he abandoned her? Had he taken this chance to run back inside? She stopped and spun around, gasping in shock when he loomed over her.

James stopped short and stared at her with a frown. "What's wrong with you?"

"I didn't expect you to be so close."

"If you hadn't stopped, I wouldn't have ended up so close."

"I was just checking to see that you were still there."

"Why wouldn't I be here?"

It was a good question, but she'd gotten suspicious because she'd barely been able to hear his footsteps. How could a man of his size walk so softly? She was certain Jackson made his every step known. "I thought you may have changed your mind about seeing my place. You'd said you wanted to."

His voice cracked. "I did?"

Ava had to stop a smile. "Yes, you wanted to see what it was like."

"But—but I thought I was just supposed to drive you home."

"To see my place. Don't you remember?" She frowned. "How much have you had to drink?"

James snapped his fingers clearly finding a way out of having to take her home. "That's right. I shouldn't drive." He pulled out his cell phone. "I'll get you a—"

She pushed the cell phone away. "You hardly drank anything, which isn't like you. Stop stalling. I'm ready to go." She walked to Jackson's car then slowed her gait when an unsettling thought hit her. What if James didn't have his brother's car keys? What if James said he'd left them inside and the brothers switched on her again? Did she really care?

To her relief the sound of Jackson's red Porsche unlocking answered her question. At least he was thorough. James opened the passenger door for her.

"It's going to be a long day tomorrow," he said.

Ava slid into the passenger seat then looked up at him. "I'm not asking you to spend the night." She crossed her legs and noticed his gaze looking at her skirt. "Unless…"

He looked away. "I think I see James—"

"No, you don't," she said impatient. If he did stall long enough, his brother would come out and ruin her plans. "Come on, you know I don't like to be kept waiting."

He hesitated then got in the car.

Ava remembered the silent car ride as she poured the coffee. Now she had him exactly where she wanted him, sitting on her couch, not knowing what to do.

His discomfort in the car had been delicious. It was even more so when he entered her apartment. Watching James playacting the role of the sexy Jackson was a study in contrasts. Although Jackson had never been to her apartment, Ava knew the first thing he would do was ask for a drink, as he checked his reflection in a glass clock she had near the door; he'd send a cursory glance at the large window, noticing the window trim and light fixtures, he liked to pay attention to details like that, before taking a seat, complaining that it was too hard, and teasing her to not take too long.

James, on the other hand, didn't notice the clock or the window, but instead noticed the hand woven rug in the middle of her living room, picked up a magazine she'd absently thrown on the floor and set it on her coffee table. He didn't take a seat until she refused his offer to help her in the kitchen and when he did, he pretended the couch was comfortable, even though it wasn't. He did it all with Jackson's flair but without his carelessness.

However, the biggest difference between the two was that James took up too much space. Jackson would have entered her apartment like a cool breeze, swift and light; James was like a humid summer, making everything feel close and tight, making her want to open a window and strip down. Punishing him came at a price because the same feeling had followed her in the car, making Jackson's Porsche feel like a Mini Cooper.

But she'd get rid of James soon. Unfortunately, not the memory of him making her two bedroom apartment feel as large as a tiny closet, so that was fine. She returned to the living room and a soft smile touched her lips when she saw him sitting with his hands gripped on his knees and head lowered like a condemned man. He obviously didn't like doing this deception. That was good, he had a conscience. But then why do it? What was Jackson up to?

Ava set the tray down on the coffee table. "Having second thoughts?"

James's head shot up and he stared at her alarmed. "No, no."

"You don't look happy."

He looked at her for a long moment. "What's with you and me being happy?"

She bit her lip, he was right. That was out of character for her. She had to be more careful and not try to push this too far.

"I guess I'm a little nervous about tomorrow."

"Tomorrow will be fine. Thank you," he said when she handed him the coffee. He moved over giving her more room on the couch. Another small slip. Whenever they went out, whether to a movie or formal event, Jackson always stayed in place. James was too considerate for his own good.

"I don't believe you."

He sipped the coffee. "Why not?"

"Because you haven't touched me all evening."

Ava inwardly smiled, biting the inside of her cheek. She could picture his mind racing for a response. *What do you say to that James?*

At first he didn't move and she wondered if he'd heard her. He stared at his coffee, he was so still she wondered if he was even still breathing. She was about to say something else when he set the cup down on the coffee table with a soft click. He turned to her and said, "I wanted to wait for us to be alone." And although that was exactly something Jackson would say the look in his eyes was pure James. Pure, unadulterated James and it was a heady sensation to be captured under that serious, penetrating gaze that dared her to look away while a hypnotic heat that seemed to fill the air around him, drew her close.

Her heart responded. She knew she should stop him now. Call him out. Throw him out. Get him out of her apartment—now. But she didn't. She didn't move, waiting to see what he would do next. She'd given him enough time alone to text his brother and get instructions on how to proceed. She expected another smooth line and then he'd leave.

"I see," she said, crossing her legs, but this time his heated gaze didn't leave her face.

He kissed her.

With no hesitation. Like a eagle swooping down to capture its prey. She'd never seen James as a predator before, but now she did. She felt it the moment his lips touched hers. A shiver of fear coursed through her as she realized she'd fallen in his trap. She'd underestimated him.

It had been a dangerous mistake to believe that his concern for his mother and brother, his soft footsteps and considerate acts were the actions of a weak man.

He was more controlled and calculating than that. His every gesture and move was not by accident, but design. She hadn't realized he'd kept her off-balance all evening until this moment when he'd been prepared to strike, giving her no recourse to deny him, claiming her as if she were his woman.

He pulled away, his voice a velvet whisper against her lips. "That's just a taste of things to come."

Another smooth Jackson line that sounded completely different coming from James. It felt like a promise. A promise she wanted him to keep. She stared at him wanting to be afraid, wanting to hate him but instead feeling aroused, excited.

She covered her mouth with a trembling hand and rose to her feet putting much needed distance between them. Rage and desire warring within her. How could he treat her like this? How could he make her feel this way?

"What's wrong?" James rose to his feet and looked at her alarmed, that same expression he'd had when she'd told him to drive her home. How could a man be deceitful and innocent at the same time?

She pounded him in the chest with her fist, not enough to hurt him but enough to release some of her frustration. He didn't flinch or even blink, he continued to look at her in a way that made her want to shake him and kiss him at the same time. "You should go."

He rested his hands on his hips and sighed. "Ava—"

"Just go."

"It will be better tomorrow. I promise." He flashed a Jackson grin. "I'm not on my A game tonight. Don't worry, I'll—"

"I'm not worried," she said in a flat tone.

"Good."

"Are you?"

He shook his head. "No. I want this."

She looked into his eyes wishing she could read his mind, but unable to hold his gaze long she looked away. "Good."

He walked to the door. "Tomorrow will be better."

She opened the door for him. "Because we'll be husband and wife."

He walked through then turned to her. "Right."

"And you'd better show up. I won't take being the jilted bride well."

"I'll be there."

"Good." She waved goodbye then closed the door. "Or there will be hell to pay."

Chapter Six

He'd briefly lost his mind. That was the only way to explain it. Between the hard couch and her soft mouth he'd gone insane and crossed the line.

James rested his head on the steering wheel. He'd made an ass of himself. He'd almost blown his cover too all because…all because he wanted to. He could lie to himself and say that he hadn't wanted her to feel unsure, especially when she mentioned him not touching her, he wanted her to feel good, but that wasn't the reason. He'd worked hard to keep her a little unsure all evening so that she wouldn't notice any differences between him and Jackson.

He'd kissed her for purely selfish reasons. He'd wanted to. He'd always wondered what her raspberry lips would taste like, the sensation of feeling the soft give of her breasts against his chest. But he'd forgotten one thing—she didn't like him.

He'd noticed the subtle signs from the beginning, how she kept her distance from him, how she gravitated towards his brother, instead of him. But if he'd been given the choice he would have offered to marry her instead.

Tonight he'd pretended she was his and he'd felt her respond to him in a way that made him crave more, then she pulled away and stared at him with a look he'd never seen before. Was it horror?

It was something that struck him to the core and for a wild moment he feared he'd exposed himself. Jackson was always free with the ladies, hadn't he kissed her like that?

He felt like a guilty fool. Indulging in a fantasy that would never be his. A woman like Ava was out of his reach, no matter how much he could pretend to be Jackson, he never would be that charming nor have the charisma. Could she tell the difference? He felt sick and humiliated that a woman would respond to him that way. Not any woman— Ava Hughes.

He still remembered the blue dress she'd worn the first time he'd met her, the way she'd quickly pulled her hand from his as if he'd burned her. He was keenly aware of her wary gaze, wondering if his initial attraction to her had been evident. He was careful, few people could tell what he was thinking, but something about him seemed to put her on edge no matter how much he tried.

But never again. He'd learned his lesson.

He'd done his brother a favor and now everything was back in place. Lusting after his future sister-in-law wasn't in the cards. She'd never know what he'd done, but it was something he'd never forget.

His cell phone rang. "Where's my car?"

James sighed, that was typical Jackson. Not, How are things? Is she okay? But, Where's my car?

He was tempted to say that he demolished it, instead he disconnected and turned the ringer off, knowing he'd have a series of messages and texts when he finally looked again.

The smell of ginger bread greeted him when he entered the family house. He had an apartment in town, but presently lived in the European style mansion. He headed for his bedroom but stopped when he noticed a light on in the library. He walked inside and saw his mother asleep on the tan leather couch, wrapped in a pink robe, her matching fuzzy slippers on the hardwood floor. James glanced at his watch, it was past eleven she should be in bed.

He grabbed a throw from the back of the chair and gently placed it over her.

"It's about time you came home," she mumbled. She sat up, running a hand through her short, silver afro.

"What are you doing up?"

She slipped her feet inside her slippers and stood. "Waiting for you to tell me what's going on."

James glanced towards the stairs.

"Don't worry, Edgar doesn't know, but he was a little suspicious."

James sighed and let his shoulders droop. "I—"

"Tell me in the kitchen."

Moments later they sat in the breakfast nook with gingerbread and a plate of sliced bananas and oranges.

"You were out late," Flo said. "Where have you been? What have you been up to?"

Kissing my brother's fiancée. "There's nothing for you to worry about."

"I will anyway. Why did you pretend to be Jackson at the rehearsal dinner?"

Damned if I know. "Jackson had a case of cold feet, but he'll be ready tomorrow."

"Poor James," Flo said, stroking his cheek. "You had to come to the rescue as always."

"Not always."

"Remember when you had to convince Jackson to finish his degree? Dump that piano teacher who was only after his money?"

"No, that was the swimsuit model."

"I thought the swimsuit model was the one with the husband."

"No, that was the lawyer."

Flo shook her head. "Your brother has terrible taste in women."

"Which is why he was panicking tonight, he thinks Ava may be one of his mistakes."

Flo looked at him for a long moment. "And what do you think?"

"I don't know." He shook his head. "I don't think so. Edgar vetted her."

"But we both know sometimes Edgar cares more about the business than the person."

"I don't think there are any skeletons in the closet. Besides, it's too late now."

"Do you think she suspected anything?"

Almost. "No." He set down his fork. "Thanks for that."

She took the plate away. "Do you want anything else?"

James sat back in his chair and watched her place the dish in the sink, a wave of sadness crushing his heart and briefly touching his eyes with tears. *Yes, please don't die. Don't be sick anymore. Give me a couple more years with you.* But he knew that was a request she couldn't grant him. The bone cancer was aggressive, the doctors—she'd visited three just to make sure—had given her six more months.

It had started as a swelling in her arm last year, followed by unexpected weight loss and fatigue before Edgar convinced her to see a doctor.

The stage III diagnosis was something none of them wanted to hear for a woman in her mid-fifties with hopes for the future.

Before Jackson's engagement, his mother had fought depression along with suffering the pain of her disease, her energy had gotten weaker, as if the cancer was taking hold at a faster pace than expected, but after his announcement she'd gotten brighter, her energy more vibrant. She'd blossomed under the thrill of working with Ava to arrange and plan everything, which was why this wedding had to take place. It was her final wish to see one of her sons married. James half wondered if Edgar had made the arrangement with Ava with that thought in mind, but doubted it. His stepfather wasn't a man known for senti-ment. However, James would make that wish come true if he had to drag his brother down the aisle himself.

Unfortunately, he didn't get the chance.

Chapter Seven

He found his brother looking resolute and defiant as he sat on the edge of his bed. Jackson rarely stayed at the family house, but had agreed to do so, so that he and James could arrive at the wedding together. James looked at the cell phone in his brother's hand.

"What are you doing?" James asked, coming into the room. "We have to leave." His mother, Edgar and Rudy had already gone ahead of them.

"I need to call Ava first."

"Why?"

He shook his head. "I'm sorry. There's something about her—"

"Just go through the ceremony. We can figure the rest out later."

"I'm sorry."

"Stop saying that."

He lifted his phone ready to call her. "I can't marry her."

James grabbed the phone before he could. "You have to."

"No, I don't."

James silently swore. "It's too late. Do you know what day it is today? It's your *wedding* day. Not a rehearsal, not an engagement. It's the main event."

"I know that."

"You have to show up."

"No, I don't."

"You can't jilt her."

"It's better than making a mistake."

"The wedding is in less than an hour," James said through gritted teeth. "And you're just figuring this out now?"

"I told you how I felt last night." He held out his hand. "Give me my phone."

"No, I won't let you do this."

Jackson stood and walked past him, heading to the door. "I'll go to her instead."

James grabbed his arm and spun him back around. "Stay away from her," he warned in a low voice. "The only moment you'll see her is when you're prepared to say 'I do'."

Jackson yanked his arm away. "That's the point. I'm not." He walked out the door and headed down the stairs. "I have to stop this."

James followed close behind. "You can't. Edgar depends on you and Mom needs this."

Jackson paused, gripping the railing. He closed his eyes. "I just feel like…" He let his voice fall away then folded his arms. "We're doing this for Mom."

"Yes," James said, pleased his brother was starting to understand the magnitude.

"Mom wants a wedding."

"Yes." He slapped him on the back. "Now come on."

Jackson didn't move, a cunning expression crossed his face. "I've got an idea."

James read the expression and frowned. "No."

Jackson held up his hand. "Just listen. It will work. You do the ceremony."

"No."

"And then we'll switch places at the reception. I'll handle everything from there." He playfully punched James in the side. "Race you to the car." He dashed down the rest of the stairs.

James ran after him. "You're crazy."

Jackson grabbed his car keys from the table in the foyer and tossed them in James's direction. "So are you."

James caught the keys then followed him outside. "No, I'm not." He pointed the keys at the Porsche and unlocked it. "I'm not doing this again."

Jackson smiled at him over the hood of the car. "Yes, you are."

"Why would I marry Ava in your place?"

"Because then the marriage would be invalid." He sat inside the passenger seat.

James got in the driver's seat and started the ignition. "And why do you want the marriage to be invalid?"

"Because I don't trust her."

"I don't care." James turned and backed the car out of the driveway. "I'm still not doing it."

"Either you do this or I tell Ava the truth." Jackson took off the yellow flower on his tuxedo, the color was the only thing that distinguished him from his groomsmen. "Either way I'm not getting married today." He reached over and pinned it on his brother's tux then patted it in place. "Just say the vows and give Mom the wedding she wants then at the reception I'll take over. Do we have deal?"

James shifted gears with force, realizing he didn't have a choice. "I'll get you for this."

James still remembered his brother's smug grin as James stood beside Ava in the church, although, to his relief, he hadn't stumbled over his vows as Jackson had during the wedding rehearsal. But his cover had nearly been blown early in the ceremony as the wedding march played and Ava walked towards him when Rudy said in a loud whisper, "But Mom, I thought Jackson was supposed to marry Ava."

His mother quietly told him to hush, but his anxious glance darted between his two brothers.

"But Mom," Rudy said, growing more agitated, "but Mom, why is James up there? Jackson's in the wrong place. We practiced this and they forgot—"

"Quiet," Flo warned in a low voice, "or I'm taking you outside and you'll miss everything. Do you want that?"

He bit his lip and shook his head but looked at James confused. James forced himself to look away feeling guilty for the look of misery on his brother's face. He glanced at Jackson who was instead ogling one of the bridesmaids in a way James never would.

Ava appeared at his side and didn't seem to have heard or noticed his brothers. He was sure if she suspected something she would stop the wedding, but she didn't, so he felt his secret was safe.

"I now pronounce you husband and wife."

James swallowed, not daring to look at Jackson as he gave her a quick kiss, knowing he had nothing to prove—everyone knew this wasn't a love match—and he didn't want to give himself away. But even the light touch of her lips against his seemed to send an electric charge through him. He made the mistake of meeting her gaze and saw them narrow a little. He smiled in a way he knew his brother would and quickly looked away. He then took her hand and led her down the aisle to the sound of joyous applause.

He smiled his way through the endless array of poses the photographer took of them, but the worse was when the photographer said she needed a picture of the couple signing the license."

"Do you really need to see that?"

"It's a very important moment," she said.

"But—"

"What's the big deal?" Ava asked. "We have to do it anyway and it won't take long."

He was going to get his fraud photographed and set in time forever. *It's okay, no one will know. No one can ever know.* He returned to where Pastor Valentine stood, the marriage license laid out on a polished wooden table. "Ladies first," he said when the pastor held out the pen to him. Ava signed with an artistic flourish, that surprised him. The constant click from the photographer's camera memorializing the moment. He would have expected a more subtle business-like signature.

"Now it's your turn," Ava said, holding the pen out to him while the sound of the clicking camera continued. How many damn pictures did the photographer need?

He took the pen, flashing a classic Jackson smile at the camera, before he signed his brother's name.

"Perfect," the photographer said pleased. "Now we can—"

"I think that's enough for now," Ava said. "There are plenty more pictures we can take at the reception."

The photographer nodded then left. Moments later, James stared out the tinted limousine windows as they drove to the hotel for the reception. Just a couple more minutes and it would be all over. He could escape this madness.

After he and Jackson switched places at the reception he'd keep his distance from Ava and try to forget this nightmare had ever happened. Maybe one day, years from now, he'd be able to laugh about it all. When the limousine pulled up to the hotel, James stepped out releasing a sigh of relief as he gallantly assisted Ava to do the same. Escape was in sight. Soon Jackson would take over, when he showed up.

Except Jackson never did.

Chapter Eight

Another damn restroom.

James paced, his polished black shoes pounding against the white floor of the empty hotel restroom.

He didn't know how much more he could take. He'd survived the thunderous applause of guests when he and Ava entered the reception hall; listened to Jackson's friend's raunchy and funny toast as people joked that James should have been giving it but had likely skipped out because he hated public speaking. Someone suggested that he'd likely be found at work instead.

James forced laughter he didn't feel. As the reception progressed he felt even less like laughing. He didn't remember what he ate, only that one plate replaced another as the various courses made their appearance then disappeared. He nursed his champagne until it was flat, his gaze scanning the crowd, looking around the room, at the entrances, waiting for his brother to make an appearance. He briefly noticed Ava's friend, Camy Hakata, was missing and remembered that Jackson had been eying her at the wedding. A thought of dread crossed his mind. Was his brother having a quickie somewhere?

Before James could give his fear credence, Camy

appeared, dashing that possibility.

After more than an hour James excused himself and disappeared into the restroom, just to have time alone to think and plan what his next move should be. He called his brother, but it went straight to voice mail. He texted him but received no reply.

James removed his ring, the flower on his tux and paced, pretending to go into a stall or washing his hands when someone else came in. After several minutes passed, he peeked his head out of the restroom but saw the hallway was empty. Where the hell was he? The church wasn't that far from the hotel. James swore and was about to dart back inside the restroom when something grabbed a hold of his ear.

"Ow!"

"What is going on?" Flo demanded, pulling him into the room.

"This is the men's room, Mom."

"I can see that. Now tell me what you and your brother are up to." She yanked hard.

James gritted his teeth. "That hurts."

"I know. I'm glad." She yanked again. "I expected more from you."

"I don't know what you're talking about."

She squeezed some more.

"Okay, okay," James said quickly. "Let go of my ear and I'll explain everything."

She released him and folded her arms, flaring out the sleeves of her pale pink dress. "I'm listening."

James rubbed his throbbing ear. "I don't know what you want me to say."

"You took your brother's place at his wedding!" She grabbed his collar. "Do you know how serious this is?"

"Mom, calm down," James said worried about her health. "I really don't know what you're talking about." He tapped his chest. "It's me. James. I was his best man."

Flo released her grip on his shirt and looked at him hesitant. "If you're James then why didn't you do your speech at the reception?"

"Nerves. I just arrived. I wanted to miss it."

She narrowed her eyes, biting her lip. "But I thought—"

"That I took his place?" James finished with an indulgent smile. "No, why would I do something like that?"

She frowned. "You did it last night."

He turned to the mirror and straightened his jacket, no longer able to face her. "That was different."

A man entered the restroom, saw the two of them then turned back around and left.

"Mom we should go."

She didn't move. "But Jackson just left the reception. Have you seen him?"

"No, like I said. I just arrived a couple minutes ago."

"Rudy thought—"

"My flower was a little yellowed, that's all. He got confused."

She looked up at him unsure. "You're really James?"

He turned to her and smiled. "Of course I'm James." At least that wasn't a lie. He held up his hands. "See? No ring. I'm still a single man."

"I could have sworn…I guess I was wrong." She placed a hand on her chest. "That's a relief."

"I'm glad."

She looked in one of the stalls. "Then where's Jackson?" She bent down to look for feet. "You're positive he isn't in here?"

James took her arm. "Mom, don't do that."

She straightened. "But if he's not in here where could he be?"

James took her arm and led her out of the restroom. "I think you should sit down. There's no need to worry. He could have briefly gone outside. I don't know, but I'm sure he's around here somewhere," he said. He kept his voice light in order to reassure her. "How's Rudy?"

"Ready to go home. You know how he doesn't like crowds."

"I think you and Edgar should take him home. You're looking a little flush."

"I'll admit that I was worried."

He kissed her lightly on the cheek. "There's nothing to worry about, Mom. You got the wedding you wanted."

Her eyes shone. "Wasn't it beautiful?" She clasped her hands together. "And oh, James, you looked so handsome and dignified up there. I wasn't sure she was the right one for you until I saw you two up there together."

"You mean Jackson. Jackson married Ava."

She frowned. "Yes, that's right, Jackson." She touched her forehead. "I don't know why I keep imagining you standing up there with her. You made such a handsome pair."

"Hmm."

She flashed a watery smile. "I guess I'm being a little greedy wanting you to find happiness."

He saw the anxiety on her face and softened his tone. "I'm happy. Now don't worry about the reception, Jackson will show up somewhere."

"Okay," She turned.

James watched her go back into the ballroom then looked around before he slid Jackson's wedding ring back on his finger. He hated lying to his mother but he knew he'd have to keep up the charade a little while longer.

Chapter Nine

J ames paused at the entrance watching Ava dance with the man who'd caught her garter. The man held her too close, taking advantage of the moment. He could understand the temptation, he'd done the same when he'd danced with her, liking how well their bodies moved together, noticing the delicate curve of her mouth, the sweep of her neck, the solid curve of her hips. James gripped his hand into a fist, he may not be the real groom, but he would keep an eye on Ava until his brother showed up.

He took a step forward, ready to reenter and make his presence known, but was stopped when a woman grabbed him and kissed him on the mouth. She then pulled away and winked. "Wow, you're right. Married men do taste different."

James could only make a noise low in his throat not trusting himself to speak. He remembered her face, she was easy to remember with dark lashes, short brown hair and a feline smile, but couldn't remember her name.

"I didn't really think you'd go through with it," she said, resting a hand on her hips, reminding him of handcuffs for some unknown reason. "You were so nervous the last time we talked."

"I'm fine now."

She let her gaze travel the length of him. "Yes, fine as always and no longer on the market."

"That's right. I'd better get back to the party."

She frowned. "Aren't you even curious what I found out?"

Found out? Jackson had her looking into something? James snapped his fingers finally placing her. Sylvia Prentiss, the cop. That's why he'd thought of the handcuffs. He remembered his brother once saying she could frisk him and lock him up any day.

Sylvia sent him an odd look. "Are you alright?"

"Yes, I'm fine. I do want to hear what you have to say, but not now."

"It's not much yet anyway. You didn't answer all my questions."

James glanced towards the ballroom eager to leave. It was either pretend to be Jackson surrounded by a crowd, or alone with a woman who was used to spotting liars. "I've got to go. People are waiting."

Sylvia smirked. "Your new bride already has you on a short lead, huh?"

His tone hardened. "No." He knew he'd said the wrong thing when he saw her face change. She looked wary. "I just need to stay away from temptation."

Her smile returned. "I know that's right."

"Send me what you have and uh…thanks for coming." He slipped out of her grasp and entered the ballroom scanning the crowd in hopes he'd see his brother.

He couldn't have left him like this. Jackson could be reckless, impulsive but not this inconsiderate. What had happened between here and the church? Had his brother gotten into an accident? Should he call hospitals?

He pulled out his cell phone to try and reach him again when it alerted him to a text.

Don't worry. I'm fine. Don't ask.

What did he mean "Don't ask?" He called him back surprised and relieved when he picked up. "I can't make it back," Jackson said before James could speak. "You're going to have to carry this out for me. Do whatever you need to." The line disconnected. He swore. His brother wasn't hurt, he wasn't dead, which was a relief, but he felt like killing him.

"I was looking all over for you," Ava said, snaking her arm around his. "I thought you were trying to make your escape."

I wish I could. "No, just catching up with people I haven't seen in a while."

"You seem to know a lot of people."

Yes, too many. "Hmm."

"I thought you could introduce me to some of them."

"Not yet."

"Why not?"

Because I don't really know most of them. "I'd rather dance," he said, pulling her into a dancer's embrace. But he made the mistake of pulling her too close, pressing her body intimately against his. He spun her away. "Better yet, let's get something to drink."

"Jackson, my man," a lanky, tall man said with a grin. "What are you two still doing here?"

He frowned.

The other man beside him sent Ava a slightly drunken leer. "Do we really need to spell it out?"

One of Ava's bridesmaid and Camy playfully pushed Ava towards him. "Yes, it's time for you two to go."

Panic gripped him. No. No, he couldn't leave yet!

Ava smiled up at him. "That's a good idea."

Nooooo!

She took his hand and said with a sly grin. "Let's say goodbye to everyone first."

His ears rang. He didn't remember his mouth moving, or his body either as she led him around the room and they thanked their guests and said their goodbyes. He felt like he was saying a different kind of goodbye—goodbye to his freedom, to his plans, to life as he knew it. There was no turning back now.

As the elevator doors closed and slowly ascended to the top floor, he felt Ava's tight grip on his hand and silently said goodbye to any chance of escaping.

Chapter Ten

The woman was a witch.

He'd sensed there was something dangerous about her and now there was nothing he could do about it. Jackson pounded his fist into the flat of his hand.

He didn't want to think about how Ava was torturing his poor brother right now. He still remembered the mistake he'd made. He shouldn't have responded to the sweet come-hither smile of Ava's friend Camy, looking alluring with her dark red lips and ink black hair with purple highlights piled high on her head. If he hadn't met her at the back of the church after his brother and Ava had driven away, he wouldn't have found himself being detained in a storage room by two guys who looked like they were straight out of a yakuza gangster film.

Camy introduced them as her brothers before they covered his face, shoved him into a waiting van and drove him to a place he still didn't know. At least they'd removed the hood.

Jackson rested his head on the locked door then turned to look at one of the large men who watched him. One of Camy's brothers. He doubted they were truly related. But the man had a hell of right hook. He found out when he tried to outwit him. They guy had actually apologized before knocking him out.

Jackson tenderly touched his cheek. Damn, what did they feed these guys in Canada?

"I don't like to miss a party so I don't have a lot of time," Camy had told him once they'd removed his hood. She sat across from him on a grey metal chair. When he opened his mouth to respond she shook her head, stopping him. "If you do what Ava wants, nothing will happen."

His eyes widened. "Ava's behind all this?"

"Of course."

"What does she want?"

"A lot of things, but first she doesn't want you to make it to the reception."

"Why not? I have to see my brother Jackson."

Camy held out her cell phone and played a recording of Ava's voice. "We know who you are," she said. "We know what you're doing and if you don't want me to destroy this precious day that means so much to your mother you will do exactly what I say."

Jackson clenched his fist. "My mother will recover."

Camy played the recording some more. "Will she recover from seeing your father's company tank? A man with a weak heart shouldn't run a business that's so unstable."

Jackson frowned annoyed that he was so predictable. "What do you want?"

Camy hit the recording again. "I want you to disappear for two days."

"No."

"Otherwise I will charge your brother with fraud right now in front of everyone. How would you like that?"

Jackson pointed at the phone. "Can't you turn that thing off and talk to me?"

Camy shook her head. "No," the recording said. "And don't get mad at her. This is your fault for trying to mess with me."

"You can't prove anything."

"All I need to do is sow a seed of doubt."

Jackson rested his hands on his hips and briefly stared at the ceiling—a dirty brown color with a single light bulb. "Where is this place?"

When Camy didn't reply, he tried another question. "How much money do you want?"

"I don't need money," the recording said.

"Revenge?"

"In time."

"For what? For this?" He threw out his hands, amazed. "The truth is I didn't want to marry you, but my brother wanted to help you save face. He's more of a gentleman than I am."

"We had an agreement."

"You're right and since he went through with it, I'll do my part. Just let me talk to—"

"It's too late for that."

He swore. "I can't believe I'm talking to a stupid recording."

"Don't try to ask for any favors. Do you think I'd let you two get together to change places again?"

"This is my mistake."

"No, you didn't do it alone. You will have to suffer equally."

Then the recording went dead.

And there was no way for him to warn his brother.

Jackson sat on the cold metal chair, imagining Camy and Ava partying like nothing had happened. He should have gone through with his initial plan and jilted her. He knew there was something strange about her. But he still couldn't put his finger on it. She didn't want money. What kind of revenge did she have in store? His mother and stepfather didn't need the stress she could cause. He'd bide his time until he could figure out what she truly wanted.

Chapter Eleven

Ava opened the door to the honeymoon suite then looked up at James with an expectant look. "Well?"

"Well what?"

"Aren't you going to carry me over the threshold?" She tilted her head. "Unless you want me to carry you."

"Oh." He swept her into his arms, trying not to be entranced by the scent of her lotion, the heat of her body. He walked forward a few feet, closing the door with his foot and scanned the room with a small sense of relief. The elegant room didn't look like a bordello—his brother would have liked that—or a romantic getaway with red rose petals, but instead it was just an impressive hotel room with soft carpeting and a bouquet of red, white and pink flowers on the wooden dining table.

The lights of the darkened city of Kirkland glittered outside the large window. He walked over to it. His brother was out there somewhere, he still couldn't understand his strange message. His voice sounded strange too. More serious than usual. Was he in trouble?

"You can put me down now," Ava said.

James glanced down, startled. He'd forgotten he was still holding her, and now he was aware of nothing else. Her face was so close to his. "Sorry," he said slowly letting her down. He had to come clean. He had to tell her the truth. He had to…

"Don't be," Ava said then kissed him.

He promised himself he wouldn't go too far as his mouth pressed against hers. Just some kissing, a little foreplay then…then he'd take a shower. Or find some way to ruin the mood. No, there was no way he could ruin this mood. Could a broke man turn away from a million dollars? A hungry man from a buffet? He wanted to push her away but couldn't.

She drew away from him with a sexy, alluring smile of invitation before she slowly turned her back to him. She slipped off her shoes then reached for the zipper at her neck. He bit his lip, eager to watch her undress, hoping she'd take her time. One part of his mind telling him to stop it, stop her, another part saying, That's right, baby. Keeping going.

If he didn't touch her he'd be safe. Look but don't touch. He was a disciplined man. A principled one and sleeping with his brother's bride wasn't the way to go. Although technically she wasn't.

She sent him a look over her shoulder. "Aren't you going to help me?"

Okay, so he had to touch her, but he'd just unzip her dress. That was all then he'd walk away. He slowly pulled the zipper down watching as her creamy dark brown skin slowly revealed itself.

"You're not saying much," Ava said.

"What do you want me to say?" James replied, his voice deeper than usual.

"I don't know."

He'd just kiss her shoulder. That's all. Then he'd stop. James pressed his lips against her skin, feeling the warmth of it and inhaling the scent of her lotion. Was it roses? Cherry blossoms?

She turned to him before he could pull away and kissed him again. He swore as her hands quickly unbuttoned his shirt.

"Did I scare you?" she said with an impish grin.

"No."

"I can feel your heart racing."

"Yes, well—"

"I like it." She kissed him again, trapping his words in his throat. She pushed him towards the bed. "You know I'm a woman who likes to take charge."

James was tempted to let himself stumble back and fall on the bed, she wasn't strong enough to force him no matter how powerful she thought she was, but he was tempted to pretend. He was tempted to let her think anything she wanted if he could feel the weight of her body against his.

However, when the back of his legs hit the bed frame, he stopped himself. If he went that far there was no turning back. He held out his hands. "Ava—"

Ava pushed his shirt off his shoulders, baring his chest, and grabbed one of his nipples between her teeth, before teasing it with her tongue. She looked up at him. "Yes?"

James briefly closed his eyes and swallowed, she was playing dirty and he liked it. He quickly moved away and turned so that he stood facing the bed while she stood with her back to it. "I need to take a shower first."

"We can take a shower later." She took off his shirt then wrapped her arms around his neck and fell back on the bed taking him with her, wrapping her legs around him. "I know you want this."

James hid a grin; she was really upping the stakes. Part of him wondered why, but another part didn't care. He did want it— her. Now. Naked in his arms, warm, wet and willing. From the first moment she came into his life he'd wanted this. He'd think about the consequences later. She'd never need to know. He'd give her a night she'd never forget. He bent down to kiss her again.

She stopped him, pressing the flat of her palm against his chest. She gazed up at him and said in a soft whisper, "I just have one question."

"What?"

Her tone turned flat and cold as did the expression in her eyes. "How far are you willing to take this James?"

Chapter Twelve

He didn't know whether he should lie or run, so he waited.

Ava shoved him away from her. "You bastard."

Yes, that was true. He blinked and sat on the side of the bed as she adjusted her dress. His heart cracked a little with disappointment at a lost opportunity, his body going from hot to cold in seconds.

"You think I wouldn't find out?" When he didn't respond she released an angry sound of frustration. "You're a fraud and a liar."

That was true too. He rubbed his forehead, shocked by how far he'd been willing to go. For a moment he didn't know himself. But he had to take control. She was upset and he had to tell her the right story to give himself some time. "Jackson was delayed. He wanted to be here and I didn't want—" He shook his head, knowing no reason made sense. "I'm sorry."

Ava jumped to her feet and glared at him. "That's it? That's all you have to say?"

"Jackson should be here any minute."

A cold smile touched her mouth. "Don't you wish."

James rubbed his fingers together. She looked mean and he liked it. "He will. My brother may come off shallow but family means a lot to him. This switch was just supposed to be for a couple hours."

"Why?"

He picked up his shirt from off the ground and dusted it off. He didn't remember tossing it there. It wasn't like him to throw things on the floor. "Cold feet, but it was nothing. I was filling in and—"

"What about last night?"

He put on his shirt, hiding a smile as he remembered Ava had been the one to put his shirt there. "What about last night?"

"Why did you switch then?"

James paused and chewed the inside of his cheek. He should be paying more attention to her. She was smart. He'd forgotten how smart she was. Somehow he'd blown his cover last night. "You knew," James said in a flat voice.

"Of course I knew."

"How? Was it the kiss?"

Ava rested a hand on her hip. "Why would I tell you that? You'd just make it harder for me to distinguish between you next time."

"There won't be a next time."

"You're right. How are you going to fix this? Our marriage isn't legal. You married me under a false name." She narrowed her eyes. "Or was that part of the plan?"

Yes. "No."

"Jackson and I had a marriage agreement. The deal was that I marry into the family. For *real*."

"No one needs to know."

"I'm so angry I'm ready to tell the world how humiliated I am. How two brothers used me like a toy. Were you *really* going to sleep with me as Jackson?"

He thought for a moment. "I-I…probably." Definitely yes.

Her mouth fell open and she stared at him for a moment, amazed. "Really?"

He shrugged and sat down on the bed. "You asked."

"And I thought you were different." She turned to the door.

James leaned back against the headboard and watched her. "Where are you going?"

"To tell your stepfather that the deal is off."

"No need to do that." He clasped his hands behind his head. "I have a new proposal for you."

She looked at him uncertain but curious. "What?"

"I'll accept my punishment. You can do whatever you want. Just wait six months."

She folded her arms. "Six months? Why six months?"

He hesitated then let his hands fall to his sides. "This day meant a lot to my mother. She wanted to see one of her sons married and I was able to make that happen. I can't see that taken away from her. I'll pay you whatever you want and after…" He hesitated, determined not to stumble over what he had to say, "after she's gone you can do what you want. Reveal everything." When he'd asked Ava if his mother could be part of the wedding preparations, he'd briefly told her about his mother's prognosis and current state of health.

Ava tilted her head to the side, studying him. "Six months you say?"

He nodded.

"That's not much of a proposal."

"Why not?"

She held up her forefinger. "Because you're forgetting one thing."

He leaned forward. "Enlighten me."

"What do I get out of this? After six months I'd still be a phony bride. I don't know if your brother will show up to even pretend that he's my husband, so why should I keep quiet?" She held up her hand before James could speak. "I'll tell you why, because I'll have what I wanted." She pointed at him. "Fortunately, you're taking me to Vegas."

He blinked, looking bored. "I am?"

"Yes, we're going to elope."

Chapter Thirteen

Ava reread Camy's initial text of Jackson's kidnapping with a smile as she sat in the plush first class airplane seat. She'd changed out of her wedding dress and wore a comfortable black pant suit with a grey colored blouse. Back to business as usual.

She remembered her friend's apprehension when she was able to slip away from the reception, into a quiet alcove to find out how her plan had worked. "Are you sure you have to go this far?" Camy asked her via video chat.

"My father depends on me. You know what the Fortunes did to him." It was also why her father was conspicuously absent. They'd decided that he couldn't attend the wedding and give her away because Edgar or Flo might remember him.

Camy's boyfriend, Tommy Park, stuck his head in the frame. "You've got to give me some love too, eh? It's not every day a Korean guy pretends to be a yakuza thug so convincingly."

Ava grinned, she'd always liked the man Camy had met in the theater department at the university. "Was he scared?"

"Tried not to show it."

She blew him a kiss. "Thank you."

"What if he goes to the police?" Camy asked.

"He's not going to report this," Ava said, certain. "I know Jackson, he'll do what I asked and you just confirmed it."

"I just think this may have gone a little too far."

"He made the move first, I'm just finishing the game."

"I hope your father will appreciate this."

I hope so too. "He will," she said used to defending her father against Camy's doubts. Camy thought Ava's father, Walter Hughes, could be overly critical and harsh, but Ava understood the reason why.

They had met through one of Ava's father's girlfriends, a distant relative of Camy. The girlfriend didn't last but a long standing friendship with Camy's family and her aunt, a Japanese woman who lived in the neighborhood and had a sort of finishing school for young Japanese adults, did. Every summer she and Camy would help entertain a group of students when she brought them to Vancouver.

Camy was more outgoing and friendly than Ava and was a successful makeup artist. Their friendship had managed to stay strong in spite of Ava's constant moving and her father's melancholy moods. Camy never seemed to be put off when Ava's father glowered in front of the TV and told them about how much the Fortunes had ruined his life.

Ava had grown up knowing that Edgar Fortune was a thief and a liar. He'd stolen her father's work, taking whatever joy he'd once had in life, and turned him into a bitter man. While her father's life crumbled, Edgar Fortune built a multi-million dollar business, leaving her father to struggle.

He'd told her how in the early days he had tried to use lawyers to get his fair share, but Edgar had defeated him before the case even went to court. No matter what battle he tried, Edgar always came out on top and untouched.

"You're the only way I can get back at him," he'd told her when she was seven. "When the law doesn't work, you've got to work outside of the law." And for the next twenty-four years he prepared her for this moment. For the moment he would finally get his revenge.

She now had the two brothers right where she wanted them. Jackson thought he was so smart, he should have known better. She wouldn't let the Fortune brothers get the best of her.

She glanced over at James as he sat looking out the airplane window. Her mind roiled with anger while her body still remembered his touch.

She still didn't know why she'd allowed her pretence to go that far. She told herself it didn't matter which brother she married. Either one would work to put her plan into action. But she knew marrying James was a gamble as bright as the lights of a Las Vegas casino. This was not what she had in mind, but it was the only option. She needed to return home with the guarantee and status that marriage into the Fortune family would give her.

Six and a half hours later she was officially his wife. They'd married in a simple and elegant wedding chapel she'd chosen. She found it embarrassing enough to have to go through an elopement with a man she hardly knew than to add insult to injury by having a gaudy décor and an Elvis impersonator, so she'd made sure to select the venue.

As she sat in the hotel room, which was decidedly, to her annoyance, even more impressive than the honeymoon suite in Kirkland, boasting floor to ceiling windows with a view of the Las Vegas Strip (she vaguely remembered James asking her on the plane whether she wanted to wake up to the sight of the strip or the mountains), and three flower vases—one on a side table in the entry way, another on the small dining table and one on the dresser. She still wondered why she was going through this.

It was a risk, but she felt that a contract would make it easier to control him. Now that she knew how deceitful he could be she couldn't be too cautious.

It was official now. The prenuptials signed (once they divorced after six months she'd be left with nothing, but she didn't care since she didn't expect to be around long), the license real. Now she could work on slowly destroying Edgar Fortune and taking control of BioMed Solutions.

Ava drummed her fingers on the dining table where she now sat, she heard James moving around in the washroom taking the shower he'd talked about before. She groaned. James. She'd married James. Unfortunately, James came with baggage that would complicate her mission a little. A dying mother and a brother with special needs, she could handle, but the fact that he lived in the family house was why she'd targeted Jackson instead. His mother wouldn't be around long enough to see the devastating impact of her plan and Rudy wouldn't understand enough to be personally hurt.

She planned to make sure he'd be provided for so she wouldn't feel too guilty about what needed to be done. The Fortunes had lived charmed lives long enough. But living in the family house with Edgar? That was never her plan and soured her thoughts.

"It's not too late to get it annulled," James said behind her.

Ava looked up, a cutting remark on her lips, then stopped when she saw him. James stood over her wrapped only in a white towel from the waist down, his well made body still damp from the shower.

She jumped to her feet. "What are you doing?"

He paused. "Talking to you."

She gestured to his towel. "I mean what are you doing like this?"

He frowned.

"Wet and half naked," she clarified, wondering if he was being dense on purpose.

James narrowed his eyes. "I bet if you think *really* hard, you'd come up with the solution yourself."

Ava folded her arms. "I know you took a shower. What I mean is shouldn't you be dressed? Don't you feel…uncomfortable?"

He pulled out a chair and sat. "Why would I feel uncomfortable?"

She pointed at him. "You're trying to seduce me."

He shook his head with a slight smile. "No, I'm not. I felt dirty and wanted to get clean."

"Oh, so marrying me made you feel dirty?"

His smile disappeared, his eyes grew dark. "Don't put words in my mouth."

"I didn't force you to do this. Jackson did and I hope you're not expecting me to—"

James rested his elbow on the table, held his chin in his hand and watched her. "You've never been seduced before, have you?"

"Of course I have," she said embarrassed he could guess she hadn't.

"Clearly by someone young, clumsy or both." His eyes captured hers, his silken tone deep with meaning. "When I seduce a woman she doesn't know it."

She believed him, that's what made her nervous. She swallowed hard determined not to show how much he affected her. She knew she would always have to be on guard with him.

"Ava, relax," he said. He freed her from his gaze by looking towards the window. "I know how you feel about me. Why do you think I reserved a room like this? I knew I would be sleeping on the couch." He returned his gaze to hers. "Feel better now?"

No. She felt too hot when he was fully clothed, now she felt like she'd jumped into an inferno. She glanced at his chest, her face burning as she remembered the feel of his hard nipple against her tongue. She shouldn't have done that. She'd hoped to frighten him a little, she'd frightened herself instead. She'd been stunned by how good it felt. "Do you sleep in the nude?"

James leaned back and casually crossed his legs. "Don't worry, I won't tonight."

Ava briefly closed her eyes not wanting to imagine him completely naked. She failed. "I mean do you normally?"

"Does it matter?"

"I need to understand your habits if we're going to live together."

"We may live in the same house, but we won't be sleeping together. Unless…" He lifted a questioning eyebrow.

"Absolutely not."

He shrugged nonchalant. "Then we'll have separate bedrooms."

"However, I still want to know if—"

"The answer is no. Do you?"

"No."

"Any more questions?"

"No."

He stared at her for a long moment then moved towards her, grabbed her by the shoulders and lifted her to her feet.

"What are you doing?" she asked as he moved over to the bed.

He forced her to sit down then stood in front of her. "Let's get a few things clear."

She smoothed down the bedspread with trembling fingers hoping he didn't notice. "I think you've made everything clear," she said in a steady tone.

"Not clear enough."

She glanced down unable to meet his gaze and noticed a droplet of water slide down his calf. "Go on."

"I'm sorry I scared you."

Her head snapped up. "What?"

He sighed. "I know I shouldn't have taken advantage of the situation in Kirkland."

"Situation?"

"The hotel."

"You call nearly sleeping with me while pretending to be your brother a 'situation'?"

"I'm trying to apologize and explain that I won't ever touch you again."

"That's not—"

He rubbed his chin, pensive. "No, that's wrong. I'll try, but you'll have to promise me not to do three things. One, don't kiss me on the mouth."

She stared at him outraged. "Why would I kiss you on the mouth?"

"Two," he continued, ignoring her question. "Don't grab my hand."

"If I—"

"And three. Don't pretend to like me. If you do, I will use it to my advantage." A glint of mischief entered his eyes. "That much I can promise you." Before she could reply he said, "Follow those rules and you're safe with me. So you can stop being jumpy."

Ava rubbed her hands together annoyed. "I haven't been jumpy."

James folded his arms and looked at her with pity.

She hated that look. She couldn't let him think she was afraid. She was the one in control now. No one told her what to do. She reached out and grabbed his hand then looked at him defiant. "I broke your rule, what will you do now?"

He pulled her roughly to him, his cold brown eyes bore into hers. She felt his wet chest dampening the front of her blouse. "Don't toy with me, Ava. I'm attracted to you, but that's not one of my weaknesses. You need me as much as I need you, but I can be scary when I want to be. I don't think you're ready for that yet." He released her.

She pulled her damp blouse from her chest, feeling hot and cold at the same time. "Was that a warning?"

"You're a smart woman stop asking dumb questions."

She didn't trust him. He could lie easily and it annoyed her that his words gave her a little thrill. The attraction was mutual, but then she remembered how he'd been able to keep her off-balance while pretending to be Jackson. He was a calculating man; he didn't say or do anything without a hidden agenda. Did it matter whether he was really attracted to her or not? She had to be careful not to underestimate him again. His attraction may not be a weakness, but if she was not careful it could be hers. "I'm still angry with you. Both of you."

James nodded. "Fair enough. But you can relax. For the next six months you'll be safe from me as long as you abide by my rules."

"Don't worry I'll follow your silly rules."

He sent her a long look. "Good and I'll do my best not to make you want to break them."

"That won't happen."

He only smiled then disappeared back inside the washroom.

Chapter Fourteen

"“This isn't what we agreed.”

Ava closed her eyes at her father's biting tone on the other end of the phone. She'd received his call on her cell phone while James was in the washroom and quickly dashed out into the hall so that he wouldn't be able to overhear her. “I know, Dad, but I had to make a quick decision.”

“Without consulting me. If you ruin all the years of planning I have put into this—”

“I won't. I know how important this is to you. Nothing will go wrong.”

“It already has. You married the wrong brother.”

“No, I can use this switch to our advantage. I now have the Fortunes exactly where I want them. This will not ruin our plans in the least, it will make it easier.”

“How can it be easier with Edgar breathing down your neck? You'll be living in his house!”

Ava leaned against the wall. “I'm sure the house is large enough that we'll rarely see each other, besides, isn't it good to get close to the enemy?”

He paused. “That is a good point.”

Ava pushed herself from the wall with renewed confidence. “I'm glad you think so.”

"But James still concerns me. Jackson had been our target for a reason."

"But James has more loyalty to his family than Jackson. Manipulating him will be a weapon we hadn't thought of."

"Another good point. Where are you now?"

"Still in Las Vegas. We'll be flying out early tomorrow morning and then let the fun begin."

"Be careful."

Ava smiled. "Always am."

Chapter Fifteen

The housekeeper, Abigail Todd, a sturdy looking woman from Jamaica with braided black hair, stared at James and Ava in confusion when she met them in the large, angular foyer of the family house. "But why didn't you call first?" she asked, taking Ava's bags from James. "I don't understand. I thought…I thought…didn't Master Jackson get married yesterday?" She touched her chest a little embarrassed. "I admit I might have enjoyed myself a little too much at the reception."

"A change of plans," James said in no mood to elaborate. "Ava's my bride now."

Abigail's face fell in dismay. "I don't have a room made up yet and have you eaten? I have to consult with the chef—"

"Don't worry," Ava said, sensing the woman's discomfort, although James didn't seem to mind, "I'm sure any room will do and I can eat anything."

Abigail looked at James sending him a silent question. He nodded in response. "Yes, you can use that room."

She smiled then nodded and took Ava's bags.

"That sounded mysterious," Ava said, following him down the hallway. "Is it a locked room?"

"It was. Clearly it won't be anymore."

"What was in there?"

He walked into the great room, a high ceiling structure that seamlessly combined the features of a traditional living and family room, and gestured to a large couch. "Would you like anything to drink?"

"No, but a tour of the house would be nice."

"Yes, I'm sure the housekeeper will show you around later. I have some work to do. I'll see you at dinner."

"But it's barely past noon."

"Let's just say I want to make myself scarce before—"

"Do you mind telling me what the hell is going on?" a voice bellowed.

James briefly shut his eyes. "But that's not going to happen," he said with a sigh. He spun around and faced his stepfather. "Let me just—"

Edgar pointed at him. "Who are you?"

James gestured to his subdued blue shirt and light grey trousers, which was in direct contrast to what his brother would wear, and said incredulous, "You can't be serious."

Edgar frowned and his tone hardened. "I'm very serious."

"I'm James."

"Where's Jackson?"

He shrugged.

Edgar looked at Ava who also shrugged.

"Why are you coming home with James when you just married Jackson yesterday?" he demanded.

Ava twisted the ring on her finger. "Actually I didn't really marry Jackson."

"What do you mean?" Edgar said, his voice rising. "We all saw you."

James cleared his throat. "Actually that was me."

Edgar fell down into a chair. "This doesn't make any sense."

"All you need to know is that Ava is now married to me."

"How?"

"We eloped."

"In Las Vegas," Ava explained.

Edgar frowned and narrowed his eyes. "Are you sure you're James? This isn't a joke?"

James nodded.

"It just doesn't sound like something James would do," he muttered to himself.

"It's all my fault," Ava said, taking James's hand. But when he gave her a low growl of warning, reminding her that she was breaking one of his rules, she quickly switched and looped her arm through his. "It happened suddenly. I told Jackson how I really felt and he helped me capture the one I wanted." She looked up at James with feigned adoration.

Edgar's keen gaze darted between them. "I see."

"I'm legally a Fortune and there's nothing to worry the stockholders and interfere with our business plans. Actually, I have a few things I want to discuss with you tomorrow."

Concern swiftly left Edgar's face. The mention of business always put him in high spirits. "Good." He stood appearing more relaxed. "I'm still confused, but as long as things are still going in the right direction I suppose it doesn't matter." He shook her hand. "Welcome to the family…again."

She smiled. "Thank you."

He left.

Ava looked up at James with a smug expression. "How did I do?"

"You almost had me fooled," James said impressed. He looked around. "Now let me see if I can escape before—"

"James, Ava, what a surprise!"

They turned and saw Flo with her arms outstretched in greeting. "Abigail just told me."

James hugged her and placed a kiss on the cheek. "It's good to see you, but I have to—"

"I knew you were up to something since the night before last." She took a seat and patted one of the cushions. "Sit down and tell me everything."

James reluctantly did, sending Ava a look that she could release his arm, but she ignored him, so they ended up sitting side by side on the loveseat. "There's not much to say."

Flo frowned in disappointment.

"I have plenty to say," Ava said.

Flo smiled, eagerly leaning forward. "I knew you would."

"The truth is, although I'd agreed to marry Jackson, I secretly fell for James. At the last minute we realized we couldn't pretend how we felt about each other so we had James and Jackson switch places."

Flo furrowed her brows. "But why did you go through the ceremony? You could have announced the change."

"Yes, I could have," James said, turning to Ava to see how she'd lie her way out of it.

"We didn't want to disappoint you," she said smoothly. "We weren't sure how you'd feel about us. So we did it for show."

James nodded. "Knowing that the marriage wouldn't be valid…"

"Allowing us to legally elope," Ava added.

"Which we did."

Flo covered her eyes.

"Mom," James said worried.

She looked at him with tears. "You're even finishing each other's sentences. I'm so happy I can't put how I feel into words." She wiped away tears. "I got to see a love match. I was so worried that Jackson was making a mistake."

James stiffened. "But you never said so. You said you wanted to see us married before…" He let his words fade away.

"I wanted to see you happy. That matters more to me than anything."

James briefly closed his eyes feeling a little sick. "But if Jackson had cancelled the wedding you would have been devastated, right?"

"I would have been disappointed, but I would have understood." She motioned to them. "Instead I got this. This is better than I could have imagined. I knew it was you standing up there. It wasn't my imagination."

"No," Ava said with a light laugh, nudging James to remove his frown and pretend to be happy.

He plastered on a smile.

Flo sat back with a happy sigh. "Thank you for loving my son. I was so worried he'd never find someone who would truly understand him."

"Yes, well…"

"You'll have to tell me more about this secret romance between you two."

"Yes."

"Later," James said. "I have things to do. As you know the housekeeper is getting Ava's room ready so—"

Flo frowned. "Separate bedrooms already?"

"Just for convenience. You know I work a crazy schedule."

"You don't have to pretend on account of us."

"I snore," Ava said.

"Make him too tired to care."

"Mom," James said embarrassed.

She stood up and winked. "You didn't invent sex, you know."

Abigail looked at Ava anxiously as Ava looked over the futuristic décor of her new bedroom, which was down the hall from James's. "It's a bit unusual, but it's one of the best rooms in the house," she said.

"It's beautiful," Ava said, although she wasn't sure that was the word to use. "If I need anything I'll let you know." Abigail nodded and left. Ava walked further into the bedroom not sure what to make of it. It was like something she'd never seen before—both beautiful and strange. The room was completely white with a touch of red accents in the pillows and curved lamp. The bed's glass backrest had a crocheted backdrop that cascaded from the ceiling like a white waterfall adding beauty and calm, the wispy bed seemed weightless as it floated near a large window. Angel soft fabric covered the bed as if the room was supposed to be a heavenly paradise.

Ava turned when someone knocked on the door. "Come in."

"Suitable?" James asked, coming into the room.

"Yes, who used to stay here?"

"Edgar's first wife."

Ava widened her eyes. "He was married before?"

James nodded. "No one knew about her. He kept her locked up in this room for years. One day she disappeared. I'm hoping the same fate won't happen to you." He shoved his hands in his pockets. "We Fortune men have our secrets."

She sent him a baleful look. "You have a very imaginative mind for an engineer."

His mouth kicked up in a grin. "I had you worried there for a minute."

"Not even."

"A couple seconds then." He sat on the side of the bed.

"But what was the room before?"

"You're really curious?"

"Yes."

"Ask the housekeeper."

"Stop calling her 'the housekeeper'. Her name is Abigail."

"Is it?" he said with little interest.

"You should at least know the name of your staff."

"Really?"

Ava opened her mouth to respond then stopped when he sent her a look and she realized her was teasing her. He had a playful side she hadn't expected.

"Why won't you just tell me?" she said.

"You won't believe me."

"Yes, I will."

"It's a guest room."

Ava shook her head. "No, it's not."

"See? I told you you wouldn't believe me."

Ava gestured to the hallway. "She—"

"Who?"

"Abigail."

He frowned. "Who?"

"The housekeeper, the one—" Ava paused when she realized he was teasing her again. "She wouldn't have given you that secret look if it was just a guest room."

"It's not just a guest room. It's a special guest room."

"Special?"

"Yes, when I want to entertain."

"I don't understand."

"That's okay." He stood. "See you later."

Unable to hide her curiosity, Ava promptly searched and found Abigail in the chef sized kitchen. "What's the story behind my room?"

"Story?"

"Yes, why is James being mysterious about it?"

"I wouldn't know. Is there something wrong with it?"

"No, thank you," she said not wanting to stress the poor woman more than she needed to. She'd figure out the true history of her bedroom eventually.

She'd been left alone the remainder of the day, getting a tour of the house and meeting the staff before changing for dinner, choosing a simple blue satin dress, although James had assured her they weren't that formal.

"What am I supposed to tell her about our secret romance?" Ava asked as she and James headed down the curved staircase to the dining room for dinner.

"I don't know what you can say about our secret romance," James said. "You're the one who came up with the idea."

"You're the one who wanted to have a wedding she didn't even really need."

"She needed something," James countered, unperturbed. "You saw how happy she is about this."

"The only one."

"Relax, six months won't be that long."

"And what if she stays so happy that she lives longer than six months?"

James sent her a sharp look and Ava felt her breath catch as she realized how cruel she sounded. "I didn't mean it like that. I meant—"

He stopped at the bottom of the stairs. "You don't have to worry. She's really dying. There won't be any miraculous cure so you'll be free in six months."

She felt wretched. She didn't like the Fortunes, but she'd gone too far. "James, listen I didn't—"

He continued down the hall. "Let's not keep them waiting."

Ava softly swore and followed him. She didn't mean to sound so callous. She liked Flo, she'd gotten to know her more working on the wedding preparations, and was a little sad that she was ill, but she had bigger things to think about.

James's love for his mother bothered her. She didn't want to care. The Fortunes had never cared about anyone. Did they care about building their wealth by stealing from others? They were users and James was only using her to please his mother. It was only fair that she'd use him in return.

Chapter Sixteen

"And that's when we knew."

Flo clasped her hands together with a happy sigh at the end of Ava's tale. "What a wonderful love story." She looked at Edgar. "Don't you think?"

He sipped his wine. "Almost sounds unbelievable."

Flo dismissed him with a wave of her hand. "He's not a romantic."

"Wonder when we'll see Jackson."

"He's probably out somewhere celebrating his freedom," James said.

"I wouldn't say that." A familiar voice said from the entryway.

Flo turned with delight. "Jackson!"

Ava stared at him. He was back earlier than expected. He had reneged on his promise to stay away for two full days. She'd hoped to have a meal with his parents without him present.

Jackson entered the room pointedly ignoring her as if the scent of the coconut rice and spiced grilled chicken set on the table had captured his attention. "Have I missed anything interesting?"

"Ava and James were just filling us in on how they fell in love," Flo said.

Jackson took a seat across from Ava as Abigail quickly set a place for him at the table. "I'd love to hear it sometime."

Flo frowned. "But I thought you already heard it since you agreed to this charade."

"Right," Jackson said quickly. "I meant I'd love to hear it again. Ava's good with stories."

"I was right," Rudy said with pride. "I knew I was right. It wasn't you up there next to her."

Jackson patted his brother affectionately on the head. "Yes, buddy."

"So where did you disappear to?" Edgar asked.

Jackson fixed Ava with a look. "You wouldn't believe me if I told you."

"Bet it included a woman," Edgar said.

Jackson nodded, filling his plate. "Oh yes. A dangerous woman. I just don't know how to pick them."

Flo nodded in agreement. "Perhaps your brother could give you some tips."

He sent his brother a secret look. "I'm all ears."

"All settled in?" Jackson asked Ava as they and James sat in the great room after dinner.

"Yes."

"Where did you put her?"

"I'm in the bedroom down the hall from him," Ava said not wanting to be spoken of as if she wasn't there.

Jackson looked at his brother and started to laugh. "Really?"

James nodded.

Ava looked at them confused. "What's so funny?"

"Nothing," James said, but Jackson couldn't remove his grin.

"Tell me about that room," she asked him.

Jackson looked at James. "Can I?"

He shrugged.

"She may get upset."

"She's already upset."

Ava scowled. "Don't talk about me as if I'm not here."

James pointed at her. "See?"

"It's his other room," Jackson said.

"Other room?"

"Yes, it's the room he used to say was his when he invited someone over, because he doesn't like anyone in his real room."

Ava looked at James. "So you lied to your girlfriends?"

He thought for a moment. "I wouldn't call it lying. It is my bedroom, just not the main one."

Jackson smiled. "And now it's yours."

Ava wanted to say something to remove Jackson's smug expression, but Flo came into the room and stopped her.

"Ava? May I see you for a minute?" she said.

She hesitated sending the brothers a considering glance.

Jackson's smile grew. "Scared we'll talk about you? Don't be. You can bet on it."

She narrowed her eyes. "Then you shouldn't be scared of what I will say to your mother."

Ava stood in triumph when she saw his smile disappear.

Chapter Seventeen

"What happened?" James asked the moment Ava was out of the room.

Jackson sighed, wishing he could tell his brother the truth. "I got into trouble with a guy I owe some money to."

"For *hours*?"

"You're lucky I'm still in one piece."

James expression changed to concern. "Do I need to do something about him? Do you need money?"

"No, it's fine. That's why I sent you the text. I'm sorry."

"That's all you've been saying lately."

"I'll make it up to you somehow. I promise."

"At least Mom's happy. Ava agreed to this charade for at least six months."

Jackson leaned back and grimaced. Six months! "That's something."

"Did Sylvia get in contact with you?"

He sat up. "Why?"

"She let me know, thinking I was you, that she's looking into Ava."

Jackson pulled out his cell phone. "I haven't gotten any messages."

"What did you expect to find?"

"Not sure, just guard your accounts."

"We signed a prenup and there will be one joint account. Everything else will remain separate."

"Good," Jackson said through tight teeth.

"You sound like you don't like her."

"I don't."

James sent his brother a searching look. "You did before. A lot. Why the sudden change of heart? I thought it was just cold feet."

He glanced up then lowered his voice. "I did too until—"

"Your mother is so sweet," Ava said, coming back into the room and taking her seat next to James. "She just wanted to make sure that I felt welcome." She looked at them. "Did I interrupt anything?"

"Yes," Jackson said.

"No," James said.

Ava nodded. "I guess I'll believe my husband."

Jackson shot her a look. "We'll see how long that lasts."

"Jackson was just filling me in on what happened after the wedding," James said, trying to ease the tension between them.

Ava lifted a brow. "How interesting. Tell me about it."

"Bookie troubles," Jackson said.

"Gambling is a vice. You should be careful."

"I plan to be. You should too."

"I don't gamble."

Jackson grinned. "I wouldn't say that."

James cleared his throat. "What am I missing?"

"Nothing."

"We're family now," Ava said. "Let's be cordial."

"We're alone. Let's not pretend that any of this is real."

"We still have to be careful," James said. "The walls have ears." He stood. "I'm heading to bed."

Ava waited for James to leave, checking the hallway to make sure no one could overhear them, before she turned and glared at Jackson. "You're not supposed to be back yet."

"I gave you enough time."

"What are you trying to do?"

He looked bored. "Nothing."

"You're making your brother suspicious."

He shrugged. "Can't help it. He knows me. We don't keep secrets from each other."

"You will this time."

"He will find out the truth eventually."

"But not yet."

"Don't worry, you're still in control…for now."

"Pull another stunt like that and I'll make my threats real. You should have seen your mother's face when I told her how much I loved her son. But if you want, I can just as easily tell her the truth." She leaned forward and lowered her voice. "You're going to be nice to me the next time we meet my dear brother-in-law." She stood and left.

Jackson watched her go, resisting the urge to trip her. He secretly hoped she'd have a tumble down the stairs or have an accident in the kitchen. He had to get rid of her some way. He'd been played. They'd all been played, his step-father the most, and there was nothing he could do about it. Yet.

But a lot could happen in six months and he wouldn't squander a minute. He wouldn't let her win without a fight.

Chapter Eighteen

A shadow went past her window. She wasn't one to believe in spirits or ghosts but her bedroom had an eerie feeling at night.

She heard something shuffle in her closet.

"Who's there?" she called out then noticed that the light in the closet was on.

She was sure she'd turned it off. She crept over to it and went inside to see if something had fallen. The closet door closed behind her. She spun around and tried to open the door, but it was fastened shut. How had she managed to get locked in? She banged on the door then screamed.

Moments later it swung open and James stood there wearing grey cotton pajamas. "What's going on?"

She dashed out of the closet and looked around the room. "I couldn't get out. Someone locked me in."

"I didn't see anything," Jackson said, coming into the room dressed in a green and black stripped robe, "and it locks from the inside."

Ava looked at him surprised; he should have left and gone to his apartment by now. "What are you still doing here?"

"It's called a family house for a reason."

Ava turned back to James. "I didn't make it up. Someone locked me in."

"Why would someone do that?" James asked.

"To scare me."

"There's no reason to scare you."

"Who would want to do that?" Jackson asked.

"Sure you don't know?" she challenged him.

James frowned. "Why would he want to lock you in a closet?"

Jackson shoved his hands in the pockets of his robe with a smug grinned. "Yes, why would I want to do that?"

Ava glared at him, knowing she couldn't share his motive without revealing what she'd done to him. It was a petty revenge, but it worked. "Never mind."

"Perhaps it was a nightmare," Jackson said. "I can relate. I feel like I'm living one right now."

"Go back to bed," James said to him. "I'll stay with her."

"No," Ava said quickly. "That's okay. I'll be fine."

"I'll stay until you fall asleep." James sent his brother a look. Jackson nodded then left.

"It's embarrassing enough," Ava said when Jackson closed the door behind him. "You don't have to do this. At least I didn't wake up anyone else."

"Hmm." James sat on the edge of the bed, like a looming dark presence in the bright white room. He looked up at her, thoughtful. "You and Jackson know something that I don't. What is it?"

Ava rubbed her arms, feeling suddenly bare in her pale blue cotton nightgown. "Nothing."

"I know Jackson locked you in the closet. He did it to me once when we were kids."

"Why?"

He measured her with a cool look. "I made him mad."

Ava shook her head. "You don't have to stay. He can try to get rid of me but it won't work."

"Why would he want to get rid of you?" James asked in a soft voice.

She'd said too much. Damn Jackson and damn James for being so observant. She searched her mind for the perfect lie. "Before I knew you'd switched places, at the rehearsal dinner I may have said something that I shouldn't have. I thought he was you after all and…" Her words trailed off.

James nodded encouraging her to continue. "And what did you say?"

"I…" She chewed her lip, hoping to look properly contrite. "I said James—you—dressed better than him. That he had the flair but you had the taste. I'd hoped you'd talk to him and convince him to tone it down a little. It's not my fault that he was really Jackson."

James nodded and Ava felt her tension easing as she watched him swallow her lie. "That would do it. His style means a lot to him."

"Yes."

"You're lucky I convinced him not to wear the red suit he really wanted to wear to the wedding."

"Red?"

"He called it crushed mauve or something, but it just looked like red to me."

Ava sat on the single reading chair that faced the bed. "That would have been ridiculous."

"It would have matched your dress."

"My dress?"

"Yes." James nodded with a faint smile. "He initially had ideas about that too. Mom persuaded him otherwise. He likes to put on a show."

"That's true."

"But it's his style that first caught your eye, right?"

Ava felt her tension return. Was James questioning her motives? She had to be careful not to criticize Jackson too much; she had planned to marry him after all. "What?"

"On the cruise. I noticed you watching him."

She blinked trying to remember. Edgar had invited her on a night cruise and she'd met Jackson for the second time, as she'd planned. But she didn't remember James. "You were there?"

He nodded.

"No, you weren't. I would have noticed you."

"Really?"

"I would have remembered if there had been two of you."

"But you didn't."

She frowned. "How could I have missed you?"

"Think back to the balcony. Did you notice anything about that moment that was strange?"

Ava let her mind drift back to the time on the cruise. She'd spent time flattering Edgar and was heady with a chance to meet his stepson again. She took a break to get away and enjoy the sea air, the breeze toying with the hem of her silk blue dress. She'd been surprised to see Jackson alone on the deck.

"How did you get up here so fast?" she asked him.

He turned to her surprised and opened his mouth, but she waved his words away. "Never mind. I don't care. It's nice to see you out of that jacket. What are you trying to be, eh? A disco ball?" She held up her hand again. "That was a rhetorical question. I know you're into fashion more than I am."

She was about to say something else, but he suddenly grabbed her and pulled her to the side just as a young man reached the railing and lost his dinner over the side.

"I guess someone had too much to drink," Ava said, wondering why she suddenly felt nervous. There was something different about Jackson, steadier, more in control. His arm around her shoulder made her body warm in a way it never had been before.

"We should get back before we're missed."

"You go first," he said.

She remembered returning to the lower deck and seeing Jackson in the hall. "Did you run here?" she asked him amazed.

"What are you talking about? I've been looking for you."

She looked up towards the stairs. "Why were you looking for me when we were just—"

"I have someone I want you to meet," he interrupted and then she forgot her confusion and pushed the incident from her mind. Now she understood as she looked at James. "That was you."

"Yes."

"Why didn't you say anything?"

"You didn't give me a chance, for one."

"For one? What's the other reason?"

He shrugged, his heated gaze holding her still. "At that moment I wanted to be him."

She folded her arms and looked away not trusting herself not to fall prey to his invitation. "You should probably go back to your room. I'm fine now."

"You haven't broken my rules yet so you're still safe."

"I don't feel safe."

He stood. "I'm a man of my word."

Ava also rose to her feet, not sure what he would do next. She wanted to be prepared. "When you're not lying."

He smiled and patted the bed. "Go to bed."

She scuttled past him and got under the covers. But the extra sheets didn't make her feel any less vulnerable. "You don't have to stay."

He took her seat in the reading chair. "I'll leave in a minute."

She closed her eyes, pretending to sleep, but when she lifted her head moments later, the chair was empty. She hadn't heard him leave.

Chapter Nineteen

For two weeks Ava studied the Fortune family, learning their habits and routines. Her days at BioMed Solutions didn't take up much attention, since her tasks were easily managed and she'd studied the entity for years, but understanding the family dynamics at home had become a new part of her plan. To her relief, Jackson stayed at his apartment. She sensed James had a hand in convincing him to leave after the closet incident, but she would never ask him.

Rudy was the easiest to keep track of. His routine was the most unchanged. A week ago he'd returned from an adult resort camp with lots of stories and presently worked hard on his business. He wanted to take the bus (for some reason he found buses fascinating), but his family provided him with a driver.

His craft business was created out of necessity and was the only opportunity for employment. Although he had achieved a university degree in History and had strong computer skills, no company would hire him for even the most basic tasks. Edgar had briefly created a position for him at BioMed Solutions, but Rudy had felt stressed and unhappy. In response, his family encouraged him to create his own business. At first he ran it online from home until he expanded to a boutique in town, which he shared with two other artists.

For the past five days he'd been moody and more aggressive than he'd been before. Because Ava had been studying everyone so closely she noticed his behavioral change first.

At dinner she noticed he wasn't eating, which was strange because food was one of his loves. His family worked hard to manage his weight knowing that obesity and diabetes were high in people with Down syndrome.

The following day, after Ava had returned from a meeting with Edgar at headquarters, she found Flo talking to Rudy in the great room. "Come work with me in the garden," Flo said to him. She had a vegetable garden on the vast property out back that she and Rudy liked to tend.

"No,"

She reached for his hand. "Just for a little while. You know I like your help."

"No," he said with more force, pushing her away. She lost her balance and fell.

Edgar pushed past Ava and rushed over to them. "What is wrong with you?"

"Honey, it's all right," Flo said quickly, taking his hand.

"Your mother is sick and this is how you treat her?" Edgar chided him. "I thought you were a grown man. That's not how a grown man behaves."

Rudy gripped his hands into fists and stared at the ground.

"Apologize."

"I'm sorry."

"Now go to your room."

He bit his lip and stomped away.

"He's usually not like this," Flo said a little embarrassed when she noticed Ava watching them. She took a seat looking worn. "But he can get into moods sometimes."

"Do you think something's wrong?" Ava asked.

"What could be wrong?" Edgar said. "He's got everything he needs and his business is doing great."

"Maybe it's me," Ava said. "Maybe having me in the house has upset his schedule."

"No, that's not it. We've had family guests before and he's fine, plus you haven't changed anything here."

"He just needs to have some time alone to calm down," Edgar said.

But Ava wasn't so sure and at dinner that evening when Rudy continued to let his food go cold without touching it, her concerns grew.

"Eat your food," Edgar said.

Rudy continued to stare at it.

"Are you feeling sick?" Flo asked.

He shook his head.

"Hey kiddo," James said.

Rudy looked at him.

"Just a couple of bites." He nodded to Rudy's plate trying to coax him with a smile from across the table.

Rudy didn't move.

"You know how I feel about wasted food," Edgar snapped. "Eat or you don't go to the next resort camp in the summer."

Rudy stared at him with wide eyes. "But I have to go. I have to."

"Then eat your food."

"We're going to Mexico and I've never been there before. You said I could go."

"Stop acting this way and behave."

Rudy took a bite of his sautéed carrots then pounded both fists on the table over and over again, rattling the dishes and shocking everyone.

James jumped up and raced over to him. "Rudy, it's okay."

He continued pounding, causing his glass to tip over and stain the tablecloth with purple grape juice.

James wrapped an arm around his brother and lifted him out of the seat. "Come on, let's go."

He screamed, but didn't fight him, tears streaming down his cheeks.

James led him out of the room.

"No," Edgar said when Flo stood to follow them, her face creased with worry. "He'll be okay."

She sank back into her seat.

Edgar cut his carrots. "I told you that we didn't need the tablecloth."

"I thought it was a nice touch," Flo said. "We usually don't but," Flo said to Ava by way of explanation. "I thought it would be nice for you."

"I don't want you to go through any trouble. I've been here long enough that you don't have to do anything special."

"See?" Edgar said. "It was a waste."

Flo's face fell.

"It wasn't a waste," Ava countered, annoyed by his cutting tone. "It was a nice gesture."

Edgar sniffed. "I'm glad you think so. Our dinners are not always so eventful."

"I've been around long enough to know how things are." She turned her attention back to Flo. "You don't have to worry. I'm not going anywhere."

"Sometimes people get frightened," Flo said, smoothing out the napkin on her lap. "But he's harmless. He wouldn't harm anyone and—"

"Stop making excuses for him," Edgar cut in. "Or apologizing. Ava knew the kind of family she was marrying into."

"I like Rudy," Ava said.

James returned to the table. Flo looked at him anxious. He offered her a smile. "He's okay now."

James wouldn't elaborate even when they were briefly alone after dinner and Ava asked him for more details. For the past few weeks they'd lived separate lives and James made no move to change that, so she went to Rudy's room on her own to find some answers. In the Fortune family, Rudy was a true innocent and she was worried about him.

She stood in front of Rudy's bedroom and lifted her hand to knock then stopped herself. *This really is none of my business. No matter how much I like him, if the family isn't worried, why should I be? James said everything was okay.*

She began to turn away, but the sound of crying caused her to pause. She turned back to the door and knocked. The crying stopped but he didn't respond. She slowly opened the door and saw him in a corner, curled up on the ground.

"Are you okay?" she asked gently, knowing it was a silly question. He clearly wasn't. He looked miserable. She walked over to him.

"I want to go to Mexico," he said.

She sat down beside him. "I'm sure you will." "But Dad said I can't because I didn't eat and I wanted to, but I don't want to."

"Why not?"

He shrugged.

"None of us like to see you so unhappy."

"Me too," he said and Ava paused when she noticed that his breath had a slight odor it shouldn't have.

"Could you open your mouth for me?" she asked.

He did.

"A little wider?"

He did and winced.

"When's the last time you went to the dentist?"

He shrugged.

She touched the side of his neck. "I don't want you to cry. You're going to get to go to Mexico with your friends and have a good time."

He looked at her with hope. "Really?"

She nodded and patted his hand. "Trust me." She left his room and gasped when she saw James standing there.

"What are you doing?" he asked in a cool tone.

"I was talking to Rudy."

"This is a personal family matter."

"Right, and I'm family."

"I overheard what you told him." James folded his arms, his eyes hard and filled with warning. "Don't make promises you can't keep. Life is hard enough for him."

Ava fought to keep her composure under his penetrating gaze. "I know that and I think I know how to help him. I was going to talk to your parents right now." She turned.

James grabbed her wrist and spun her back to him. "You can tell me first. I don't want you upsetting my mother either."

"She needs to hear this. I have an idea." Ava sent a pointed look at his hand on her wrist. Do you mind?"

He released her and said in a low voice, "Your idea had better be a good one."

Chapter Twenty

"A dentist?" Edgar said, doubtful.

"I'm not a doctor," Ava said as she sat across from him in the library. Flo sat quietly beside him and James stood by the wall. "But I think there might be something wrong with his mouth. That's why he's not eating and being miserable. I also detected some swelling under his jaw."

"We have to schedule him right away," Flo said, her voice anxious.

Edgar frowned. "There's no need to panic."

"I could be wrong," Ava said.

Flo took out her cell phone and checked her calendar. "For his sake, I hope you're not."

The dentist discovered Rudy had a major abscess that needed to be expressed. Once it was taken care of Rudy was back to his old cheerful self giving Ava a big hug when he returned home from the procedure and found her waiting to greet him in the foyer. "I get to go to Mexico like you promised, Dad said I could."

"I'm glad," Ava said with a smile.

"And I want you to have this." He pulled a sterling silver necklace with an amethyst pendant from his pocket.

"Oh, it's beautiful."

"I know. I made it. Let me put it on you," he said, unclasping the latch.

"But it's too pretty to wear now," Ava said, looking down at the unflattering pant suit she wore.

"You can wear it with anything." He draped it around her neck.

"Are you trying to make moves on my woman?" James said, coming down the stairs.

Rudy giggled pleased.

"It's the nicest gift I've ever gotten," Ava said.

Rudy gave her another hug, kissed her on the cheek and said, "I love you," before heading to his room.

"Thanks," James said.

"I wasn't pretending," Ava said, staring down at the necklace. "I really do like the gift. No wonder your brother's business is so successful. Just wait until Camy sees this."

James shook his head. "Not about that, about what you did for him."

"It was nothing," Ava said suddenly feeling shy.

"No, it wasn't. He's not articulate and sometimes things like this get missed. It could have been worse." He paused. "I'm sorry I doubted you." He looked at her for a long, powerful moment, desire clear in his gaze. She felt it too, a longing to touch and taste him again, wondering how she could close the gulf that had come between them. But she knew that keeping him at a distance was the only way to keep her traitorous heart safe. She could care for Flo, even for Rudy, but caring for James could destroy her.

As Ava had predicted, when she sent a photo of her necklace to Camy, her friend wanted one of her own and promptly went to Rudy's website and ordered two, as did a number of her friends until the design was sold out.

To Rudy's delight, that Saturday, Ava came and visited his boutique, which was located on a side street lined with other high end specialty stores. He showed her around the exquisitely decorated bright room and shared some of his other ideas.

She treated him to lunch, remembering Flo's warning that he wasn't allowed to overindulge, then after returning him to the boutique, left him to go run some errands.

She was halfway to her car when she saw Edgar across the street, standing near his black Mercedes in front of a nondescript building. At first she thought he was coming to pick Rudy up, since there were no stores in the vicinity that would interest him, then she noticed a woman in a flowing yellow dress step out of the passenger side of his car. The woman was probably a decade younger than Flo with light skin and medium length brown hair.

Ava scrambled to get her cell phone from her handbag and took a picture as he and the woman hugged in a manner that was far from professional. Such evidence would come in useful eventually. Her heart turned cold as she watched the pair disappear into one of the stores.

She looked down at the photo of them embracing. This was the reminder she needed. This was why she was here and why she needed to focus solely on her task. Edgar was a true bastard. He had a woman on the side while he had a dying wife at home. Ava put her cell phone away, her heart breaking for Flo. She couldn't be swayed by his care for Rudy or the image he liked to portray to the world. This was the real him. He deserved to go down.

Chapter Twenty-one

"You're still acting like a single man," Flo said as she placed a basket of lettuce, okra and red bell peppers she'd picked from her garden, on one of the two islands in the large kitchen. The smell of the spring day seemed to follow her with the scent of sunshine and fresh soil.

James looked up from his position at the kitchen table where he'd been reviewing the data of one of his projects. "What?"

"Ava doesn't seem to be comfortable here and I rarely see you two together. After what she did for Rudy she should feel like she's part of the family now, but you two act like strangers. You live different lives."

"You know we married for business reasons. Edgar's happy that—"

"I thought you married for love."

James paused; he'd briefly forgotten *that* part of the story.

"She knows I love her," he said pleased he didn't stumble over the words. "She's fine."

Flo took a seat in front of him. "Have you asked her?"

He sighed. "Mom, trust me. We're happy."

"That's how marriages fail. It's because the man is clueless. Show her some affection. Your brother Rudy is more affection than you are."

"He always has been."

"It wouldn't hurt to show a little tenderness once in a while."

"I do…you just don't see it."

"Hmm," Flo said, but she continued to worry that her son was neglecting his new wife. It had been nearly a month and she sensed something was amiss between them. Perhaps they'd had a martial spat early on and neither one wanted to address it. She knew she had to do something before it got out of hand.

She found Ava reading in her bedroom. Her new daughter-in-law was almost always there only coming out to be with the family at dinner. She never ventured to the back patio or even the library, which Flo thought would be much more comfortable. She knew Ava had grown up as an only child, but found it strange that she didn't feel comfortable using any other rooms in the large house.

"May I talk to you?" she asked.

Ava set her book aside. "Sure."

Flo hesitated then sat on the bed. "I'm sorry James put you in here."

"I like it."

"Really?" Flo shivered a little. "I find it so cold. Distant."

"I like the minimalistic lines and lack of color."

Flo laughed, pleased. "I guess that's why you fell for him."

Ava frowned not understanding her response. "What?"

"James." She gestured to the room. "This was one of his projects."

"Yes," Ava said in a grim tone. "His special guest room. I'm surprised he told you about it."

Flo sent her an odd look. "Why wouldn't he?" Before Ava could respond, she grinned, "Have you tried the bed out yet?"

"The bed? Of course. I've been sleeping on it."

"No, I mean really tried it out. Didn't he tell you that he had this room designed for me?"

"No," Ava said, drawing out the word. "He lied and said…" She shook her head. "Never mind."

"He didn't tell you the truth?" Flo said surprised.

Ava shook her head.

She sighed with regret. "It's probably because I hurt his feelings. I didn't mean to."

"I don't understand."

"After my diagnosis James had this room redesigned for me hoping for a calm sanctuary that would help me heal. He made the bed appear weightless so that I could feel as if I were floating and the view from the window changes with controls and the bed…" She shook her head.

Ava leaned forward curious. "What about the bed?"

"It actually frightened me."

"Why?"

"It's attached to a mobile device and embedded with software that knew too much about me. When you lay down it is programmed to adjust to your body temperature, read your heartbeat, adjust to the curve of your body, it even comes with a virtual reality headset. Want to try it?"

"Okay," Ava said uncertain.

Flo pushed the side of the bed frame, opening a hidden drawer. She pulled out the headset and gave it to Ava. "You wouldn't believe how long it took me to figure this out." She watched Ava put on the headset then said, "Are you ready?"

"Yes," Ava said. Seconds later a hillside landscape, lush with greenery, seemed to surround her. "Oh, it's lovely." She looked around at the clear sky feeling as if she could touch the green grass beneath her feet, then a dark shadow rose from behind one of the hills. As it raced closer, she felt the ground beneath her feet move and soon the shadow gained form. It became a large monster with black fur, seven eyes and razor sharp teeth inside a black foaming mouth. Its eyes pinpointed her as if ready to eat her alive. "What am I supposed to do?"

"Grab the sword."

"There's a sword?" Ava asked, frantically searching for it until she found it down by her side. She struggled to pull it from its sheath as the creature continued to come closer "Why didn't you tell me before?"

"It's been a while. I forgot."

She held out the sword. But it seemed like a twig in comparison to the monster, but she still used it to try to slice the monster before it got any closer. "It's not scared," she said noticing that the monster's pace hadn't slowed.

"You have to kill it. Quickly."

Ava reached out and tried to battle the monster, but it jumped on her and opened its large dark mouth, salvia dripping down as it prepared to sink its teeth into her neck. She screamed and tore off the headset. She stared at Flo, her heart racing. "What was that awful thing?"

"The cancer. James worked with a friend to develop a game to help patients find an outlet to fight their diseases. Unfortunately, his monster is too real."

"Perhaps for true gamers it would be better." Ava wiped sweat from her forehead. "It's not too bad if I'd been more prepared."

"It was scary."

"Terrifying," Ava admitted, handing Flo the headset. "But still impressive. Perhaps if he changed the look of the monster or created different levels and gave people the option as to whether the bed would also move or didn't, as if you were there, then it would be better."

"Maybe, but after one moment in that world and on this bed, I had nightmares in this room and never returned. I prefer my meditation and yoga."

"And your gardening," Ava mentioned with a smile.

"Yes."

Flo hesitated then said, "I'm telling you about the bed so that you can understand that James means well even if he doesn't show it the way he should."

"I know."

She took Ava's hand and held it between both of hers. "You joined our family just in time. When I think of what could have happened to Rudy if you hadn't—"

Ava touched one of Flo's thin shoulders. "It's okay."

Regret made her eyes sad. "If I hadn't been so tired I would have paid more attention. I used to worry about Rudy. We have him taken care of financially. Edgar promised me he'd do everything he could." The sad look left her eyes, replaced with joy. "But now I know Rudy has someone like you also looking out for him and it puts my mind at ease."

Ava hugged her hoping Flo would never really know the truth about her husband.

Chapter Twenty-two

Flo left Ava's room and lay on the bed in the master bedroom, sweeping her hand over the plush bedspread; she closed her eyes remembering when she had felt like a stranger in the elegant room.

Neither she nor Edgar had married for love. And in the beginning they had separate bedrooms and lives, much like Ava and James, only coming together when Edgar requested her company. Flo didn't expect much else.

And for five years they lived that way until one night after they'd been together, Edgar said, "It's late, you can stay."

Flo halted halfway out of the bed not sure she'd heard him correctly. "What?"

"I said you can stay."

Flo hesitated not sure she wanted to. At first she'd dreamed of being a true wife to him, of turning their formal arrangement into something more, but over the years he'd made it clear that wouldn't happen. But now this. She stared at his hard profile; he wasn't a man to jest. She cautiously slipped back into bed, gripping the bed sheets to her chest, not quite sure what to do.

He sighed annoyed. "You don't have to stay if you don't want to."

"I do." She swallowed, releasing her grip on the sheets. She glanced at him again before she reached and turned off the lights.

"Are you happy?" he asked, his voice sounding deeper in the darkness.

What a strange question to ask. "Yes," she said not sure of his strange mood.

"And the boys?"

"They are happy too. You fulfilled your promise."

He didn't reply and she didn't expect him to. She'd gotten use to his silences. She bit her lip and inched closer to him. When her skin touched his, she closed her eyes and waited, wondering if he'd turn or push her away. Instead he drew her closer, his arm felt warm and solid around her. He pressed a featherlike kiss on her forehead. "You can stay every night if you want."

It was then that their relationship changed, that she finally understood him. He wanted her to stay, but he'd never admit it. She searched her heart, amazed by how buoyant and happy it felt and realized that he was no longer a stranger to her; she could accept him fully as her husband. Until that moment she hadn't realized how much she wanted to.

"Do you want that?" he asked.

She nodded and whispered, "Yes." And she stayed for the next twenty-three years.

Flo opened her eyes and looked around the bedroom with a smile that slowly faded as she thought of the fate that awaited her. Was it fair to him to keep sharing this room? This room filled with memories of their marriage? She glanced at the beige wingback chair where Edgar had stayed for hours after his uncle died; the window where they'd stood arguing about Rudy's future. She had initially been against Rudy starting his own business, but Edgar had been adamant and she was glad she'd listened, but it had taken a lot of persuasion on his part.

She'd had more fight in her back then. Others had been afraid of him, but not her, although she never let that truth show in public. She was keenly aware of Edgar's reputation and wouldn't do anything to jeopardize it, but in private she could be fierce and knew he secretly enjoyed it.

But she wondered if he took any pleasure in her anymore. Her weight loss had stolen some of her beauty; her energy wasn't what it once was. Did he at times regret his decision? Did he sometimes want space?

She'd once broached the subject about moving into another room, but he'd swiftly dismissed the idea and she'd never brought it up again. However, she knew there would come a time when they wouldn't be able to share a room or a bed and she wondered how she would be able to bear it.

Chapter Twenty-three

"You lied to me," Ava said when she found James on the large, curved back patio, listening to the tranquil sounds of the water rippling from the pool below.

James turned a page of the report he was reading. "I know."

"About the bedroom."

"Oh, that." He briefly looked up at her. "I didn't lie. Jackson did."

"You went along with it. And at first you said it was a special guest room."

He nodded in agreement. "It sounded more interesting."

"You could have told me the truth."

He closed the report and sat back in his wooden chair. "That I created something that gave my mother nightmares for weeks? I don't think so."

"Weeks?"

He opened the report again.

Ava sat in front of him. "I was telling her that if you changed the look of the monster you may be on to something."

"You think so?" he said sounding bored.

"I like how it corresponds with the bed."

He shrugged. "I've moved on."

"I can't believe you designed that bedroom. I always wanted a floating bed."

He looked at her surprised. "Really?"

"Yes, ever since reading—"

He shook his head. "Don't say it."

"*Robot Chronicles.*"

He closed his eyes as if in pain. "I can't believe you said it."

"Why?" Ava said perplexed by his response. The books were very popular in her childhood and considered classics now. "Didn't you like the series?"

"Couldn't stand them," James said with feeling, "but Jackson had to read every single one."

"My father didn't let me read them so I had to sneak them. He said they were filled with junk science."

"He was right."

"That's why it's called *fiction* and the storytelling was amazing."

James returned to his report. "I'll have to take your word for it."

"Have you tried the bed yourself?"

"No."

"You should."

A slow smile spread across his face and he lifted his gaze to hers. "Is that an invitation?"

Ava cleared her throat, feeling suddenly warm. "I mean you should try it after I'm gone."

"Oh," he said sounding disappointed. "That doesn't sound as much fun."

"What doesn't?" Jackson said, stepping through the sliding glass doors to join them.

"Nothing," Ava and James said in unison.

Jackson took a seat and sent them a suspicious look.

"I found another fan of those boring books," James said.

Jackson frowned. "Boring books?"

"*Robot Chronicles.*"

"What do you mean *boring?* Those were the best."

"I know," Ava said.

Jackson looked at her amazed. "You liked them too?"

"They got me through school."

He stood and did the mock salute of one of the characters. "Are you ready to serve?"

She stood and did the same. "All the time all the way." She clapped her hands then pointed to the sky.

Jackson laughed, impressed. "You remembered that?"

"Of course. I disappeared into those books as well as my manga collection."

Jackson snapped his fingers. "Oh right. I still have one of your *Fullmetal Alchemist* copies. Volume–"

"That's okay." She'd loaned it to him when they were dating. "I started another series set in a post-apocalyptic world where humans live inside cities surrounded by these enormous walls."

James shook his head in mock dismay. "How old are you two?"

"Good stories know no age."

"Comic books."

"They are not—"

Jackson waved his hands. "Don't try to convince him. He doesn't get it."

James smiled. "Something else you two have in common."

"Something else?"

"Yes, I know you're both sharing a secret."

"No, we're not," Ava said when Jackson looked away.

James shrugged, nonchalant. "I'm not worried. I will find it out." He nodded at his brother. "What are you doing here?"

"Stopped by to see Mom and Rudy." James looked at Ava. "Heard what you did for him."

"Yes," James said. "I guess we're lucky to have her."

Jackson rested his elbows on his knees and smiled at her. "You'd like us to think that, wouldn't you?"

Ava stared back at him determined not to be provoked. "I don't care what you think."

"How come there's not much about your life before Canada?"

"What?"

"Are you looking into her background?" James asked.

Jackson kept his gaze on Ava. "Just curious."

James lowered his voice. "We're doing this for Mom. There's no need to stir up trouble."

"We're already in trouble."

"What does that mean?"

"It means that I hold all the cards and he doesn't like it," Ava said, stopping Jackson from saying anything else.

"Could you excuse us for a minute?" James said then shook his head when she opened her mouth. "I'm not really asking."

She shot Jackson a dirty look before she left.

"You're doing it again," James said once she was gone.

"What?"

"Every time you're around her you go for the jugular. What is going on?"

"I just don't like this set up."

"It's working right now. Mom is happy and so are Edgar and Rudy."

"And what happens to Rudy and Edgar if something happens to us?"

"What could happen to us? I'm the one who committed the fraud. If she wants to bring up fraud charges against me for what I did, I'll face the consequences. It has nothing to do with you. Until that time I'm trying my best to make this work."

"Maybe I don't want it to work," Jackson muttered.

"You're not making sense. Ava and I have an agreement. We keep this up and then we'll get a divorce and I'll—"

Jackson shook his head. "You're going to have to do more than that. She's been meeting with Edgar a lot lately and her interest in the company is intense. Almost obsessive."

"It always has been." James sat back and studied his brother. "I know she's up to something if that's your concern."

Jackson rubbed his chin. "But what and why? We have to do something."

"Like what?"

"Her life begins at age three in Canada. Don't you think that's strange?"

"I really don't care."

"It means she's keeping secrets."

James drummed his fingers against his knee. "What do you want me to do about it?"

"We need leverage. She's winning over our family."

"And what's your solution?"

"You have to make her fall for you."

James laughed. "I can't make that woman do anything."

Jackson sent his brother a hard look. "Yes, you can. I've seen you do it before."

James's good mood died. "That was different." He'd used his limited charm in the past to get what he wanted.

Only his brother knew that his past breakups had always been strategically designed so that the other party felt that they had made the decision.

"I think you've let your guard down and have forgotten what this is really about."

James shrugged. "I'm willing to listen. What is it about?"

"The two things Edgar taught us were important—business and power. If we continue to stay in control we keep the upper hand."

James sighed. "Why do I get the feeling that you have something in mind?"

"Because I do."

James motioned him forward. "Go on. Tell me."

"You've got to up the stakes and steal her heart."

Chapter Twenty-four

James didn't argue with him.

Jackson took that as a victory when his brother left the patio and returned inside. He closed his eyes and rested his head back, letting the sun warm his skin. He'd lied when he'd told his brother why he'd come to the house. He'd really come to see how Ava would respond to his questions about her past. A smile touched his mouth as he thought of how he'd gotten the information he needed from Sylvia.

"You call that a quickie?" Sylvia demanded when Jackson rolled away from her and grabbed his jeans from where he'd tossed them over the couch in her apartment. "That was barely even a second."

He playfully slapped her on the bottom. "What do you have for me?"

She pulled a face. "How come you always make me feel used?"

He zipped up his jeans and winked at her. "You like being used."

She pulled on her large T-shirt, which she found crumpled on the ground. "We could make a great—"

He shook his head. "It would never work."

She pushed away an empty can of soda and a bag of caramel popcorn with her foot and reached for her skirt, brushing off some dust bunnies that clung to the pale, worn fabric. She should have cleaned up before he arrived, but she hadn't known he was coming until he was halfway there and she didn't want to turn him down. "It's not like you to be afraid of commitment."

"I don't trust my taste in women." He sat down beside her and nudged her with his elbow. "Present company excluded."

She pulled up her skirt. "Thank you."

"But I'm on a fast. No commitment for the near future."

"And what do you have against Ava?"

He playfully tweaked her chin. "Tell me what you found."

Sylvia sighed, knowing he wouldn't tell her. She liked him unfortunately their timing was always wrong. She'd first met him when she was still married to the man she fondly liked to call Her Greatest Mistake. By the time she divorced, Jackson had gotten burned twice and then fallen for Ava.

Although his relationship with Ava was now over, she suspected Jackson was right; she and he would never last. He had another side she couldn't reach, but she knew she'd enjoy herself in the meantime.

"I don't know why you need to use a lowly cop like me when your father likely has bigger fish on the hook to get the information you want."

He affectionately kissed her on the cheek then said, "Tell me."

"Not much. She has no past starting in Canada."

"What do you mean?"

"I mean that she doesn't have anything before the age of three. Her life before that is nowhere."

"That's impossible."

"Not if you know what you're doing."

"But—"

"I think I might know why," Sylvia interrupted, "but I can't tell you yet until I'm sure. I don't want to accuse someone of something until I have more evidence."

Jackson tapped his finger against his knee, pensive. "Is it big?"

"Could be."

"I knew it."

"Or it could be nothing so don't jump to conclusions. But if it is something, she was a child and may not know anything about it either. It could surprise her."

"I don't care," Jackson said in a grim tone.

"You should. She's married into your family, right?"

"Don't worry. I'll make sure that James and Ava don't stay married for long…"

James and Ava. He didn't like how cozy they'd looked together on the patio and he remembered the excited voice of his mother telling him how much she liked Ava and all that she'd done for them. Jackson opened his eyes and stared over the vast property, lingering briefly on his mother's vegetable garden. If James did what Jackson told him to, Ava would regret she'd married him in the first place.

Chapter Twenty-five

His brother's idea was just as ludicrous as wanting to switch places, James thought as he poured himself water from the fridge. He'd fallen for Jackson's idea once—no twice!—he wouldn't do it again. Even though it was tempting. He knew Ava responded to him and it would be fun to see how he could manipulate her.

But they had an agreement and their arrangement worked for now. For the past several weeks they'd been cordial and he'd managed not to think about her too much. She stuck to his rules and he stuck to his cold showers.

Lots of cold showers. Like the one after he saw her in the garden, running her hand up and down an okra's short stem, or at the dinner table when her legs brushed against his. His work kept him busy and that would be enough for now. James finished his water and left the kitchen.

"She's alone right now," Flo said, grabbing James's arm as he passed her in the hall.

"Who?"

"Who else?" she said with impatience. "Ava. I convinced her to sit in the library."

He frowned not understanding her reasoning. "So what?"

"Go to her."

"Why?" James asked, letting her drag him towards the library so she wouldn't expend too much energy. "I don't have anything to say."

"Make up something. Sit with her for a minute."

"And do what?" he asked just to tease her. He found the situation amusing. His brother and mother both wanted him to do the same thing but for different reasons.

"Do I have to tell you?"

James peeked into the room. "She's reading. She probably wants to be alone."

"Go and put your arm around her. Ask her how she is."

"Mom, I really don't—"

"You're going to lose her at this rate. I may not be around to see any grandkids but I would like to believe in the hope there's a possibility." She shoved him forward. "Go."

James stumbled into the room and offered Ava a look of chagrin when she lifted her head in question. "Sorry about this," he said in a low voice, taking a seat beside her. "Just pretend to be happy to see me, my mother is watching."

Ava caught a glance of Flo before she disappeared behind the wall.

James stretched his arm behind her head. "Don't stiffen like that I'm only doing this until she goes away."

"I'm not stiff. What did Jackson say about me?"

James frowned down at the book in her hands. "What are you reading?" He leaned forward. "Is that—?"

She slapped him in the stomach with the back of her hand. "Shut up."

He looked at the manga graphics. "The drawings are impressive."

"I said shut up. I don't want to hear your comments on my reading material."

"There aren't many words though."

"Be quiet, James."

He slid his arm to her shoulders and lowered his voice, "I either keep talking or I kiss you. Your choice."

For a moment Ava didn't move, not sure how to respond.

James pointed to one of the illustrations, the movement bringing her body closer to him. "I really like that one."

Ava bit her lip, resisting the urge to lean in. He smelled good. But what had he and Jackson talked about? Why had Jackson brought up her past? Was James here because of his mother or for another reason?

She looked down at his free hand resting on his lap, swallowed and made a bold decision. She covered and held it.

This time James didn't move, but his voice deepened. "You're breaking the rules."

"I know. What are you going to do?"

His mouth covered hers.

And she totally forgot about Jackson. Or breathing. His mouth left hers burning with fire. Then she felt his tongue, not sure if she'd made the initial invitation or not, but surrendering to its persuasion. Her hands reached for him.

"Hold on," James said, waking her from her dream. She looked down and saw that she'd unbuttoned his shirt. "Your bedroom in two minutes."

"Why not yours?"

He pressed a finger against her lips. "I'll make it one. Are you scared?"

She searched his gaze, her heart racing, realizing what she faced. What she'd done. She should be horrified. She'd lost herself. Her dignity. Her inhibition.

She didn't care.

She wanted him and he wanted her. She jumped to her feet and ran.

Once she reached her bedroom she quickly searched it to see if there was anything visible that would ruin the mood, but it looked fine. She didn't know if she should strip down, let him undress her or do it herself.

She covered her face and made a sound of frustration. No, she couldn't have these questions. She had to get back in control. If he knew how much he could dazzle her she would be at a disadvantage. This was just sex. Nothing more. She didn't really like him, just wanted him. A lot. More than a lot if there was such a thing. She was a straight, healthy woman with a handsome man who wanted to sleep with her, she was not making a mistake.

It was just physical. It didn't mean anything. So she was attracted to him, that didn't mean it had to be anything serious. For weeks she'd been secretly lusting after him, and now she could finally get him out of her system.

Chapter Twenty-six

James didn't know what to expect, but the sight of Ava in a pair of heels wearing only black lace panties and bra wasn't it.

He wasn't sure how to read her expression. She was up to something but he wasn't sure what. He slowly closed the door behind him and removed his shirt. "You don't waste any time," he said, placing it over a chair.

"No." She walked up to him and tugged on the waist of his trousers. "I like it quick, hard and a little rough. Think you can manage that?"

James smiled, finally understanding what she was up to. "Yes." He removed his socks and shoes and placed them together near the chair.

She frowned. "What are you? A neat freak?"

"Is that a problem?"

"No." She folded her arms. "So you know what to do."

He nodded, removed his trousers and placed them over the chair as well.

"Good."

"But I don't take orders."

She paused. "What?"

He cupped her chin in his hand, his eyes dark. "Somehow you've confused me with someone you pay for."

She removed his hand. "Do you want to sleep with me or not?"

"I will sleep with you tonight," he said, his voice holding a note of promise, "but on my terms not yours. Remember you broke the rules."

"But you're the one who's scared," she shot back, meeting his eyes. "Scared you can't handle a simple request from a woman like me."

He sniffed. "A woman like you?"

She nodded.

"What makes you so different?" he challenged, taking an aggressive step forward, inwardly pleased when she took a step back. "Do you think you're my first? Do you think you're somehow special?" He took another step forward; this time she held her ground, but not for long. "Is that what men have been telling you? Have they been telling you that you're so strong and independent that you frighten them?" He held her gaze. "Do I look frightened?"

She turned away. "You can leave—"

"I can see through it all, Ava. I can feel how you respond to me. Is it fear or something else?"

Ava hugged herself, annoyed that he'd been able to intimidate her. She shouldn't have backed away no matter how uncomfortable he made her. He was too close to the truth, but if she wanted to control him he couldn't know that. She forced herself to look at him again. "It's not fear. I just don't—"

"Want to be alone with me too long?"

Yes. "I like my space."

He swept her with a considering look, his gaze feeling like a heated caress over her body. "You want it quick, hard and rough?"

She nodded, not trusting herself to speak.

"You're sure?"

"Yes." She knew it was a challenge and didn't expect him to do it right. Most men didn't. If he did what she expected him to—try to prove himself, his manliness and power—he'd be another unmemorable bedfellow to ease some frustration. And she always liked a little pain with her pleasure; like salt and sugar on popcorn. She hoped to end up with some bruises, maybe a tiny scar. She wondered if he'd use his teeth, scrape her skin with his nails, grab her throat and squeeze.

But he tricked her, not in the way she expected. He was quick—having her naked and on the bed within seconds—and he was hard, big and solid as he entered her. He was also rough—she felt the raw passion of his entrance as she prepared herself to ride him into climax, but then he slowed the pace and kissed the curve of her neck.

"What are you doing?" she asked with a note of panic.

"A compromise," James whispered, his breath hot against her skin.

"But I said I wanted it rough."

His eyes captured hers. "I can be rough and smooth."

And to her surprise he showed her how.

Making himself memorable in the most wonderful, exciting and frightening way. He wasn't a quick lay she could forget, he made an imprint and she was helpless to stop him because as much as she wanted to pull away, she craved more. No man had ever taken so much time to explore her body, to find her pleasure points, to touch her so tenderly, but also with reckless abandon. She didn't think he had it in him. She'd been wrong. She'd offered him a challenge and failed.

But what a glorious defeat.

She knew once wouldn't be enough, even when he stopped she craved more.

She'd never known the true pleasure of a man's tongue before, the feel of it between her toes, against her navel, touching the tip of her center with wet, warm delight, leaving her languid with desire.

It wasn't supposed to be like this.

She wanted it to always be like this. She enjoyed him with equal hunger, dragging her nails down his back, tightening around him, inviting him deeper inside her. She wanted to devour him, using her teeth against his chest, wondering if she could frighten him a little. It only seemed to excite him more and that thought—that she couldn't scare him—thrilled her and she knew she was in danger of falling in love.

James lay on his side and looked down at her. "Well?"

Ava turned her head on the pillow and stared up at him. "Well what?"

"Did I succeed?"

She frowned. "You know you did, smug bastard."

He smiled. "Just wanted to make sure."

"Where did you learn to do that thing with your tongue?"

He bit his lip. "I probably shouldn't tell you this."

"Why not? Embarrassed?"

"A peach."

She blinked. "What?"

"A peach. My brother and I used to practice on a peach. We'd cut it in half, remove the pit and do the rest. An older cousin of ours told us the sensation was kind of the same." He winked. "Warm, sticky, sweet."

"I don't believe you."

He shrugged. "It's the truth. I haven't had any complaints yet."

"You must like peaches a lot."

He only smiled.

"Clearly you've perfected your skill."

"Glad you noticed. I would hope I would be better than I was at eleven."

She sat up and stared at him shocked. "You were doing that to peaches at eleven years old?"

"Late bloomers I know."

She pulled the bed sheets to her chest. "You're making this up."

He shook his head. "No, it's the truth. I tried plums once, they were a disaster. And forget about the kumquat. I'd gotten too ambitious."

"Horny little bastard."

He grinned.

She rested her head on the pillow and pulled up the sheets. "I'm ready to go to sleep."

"You'll miss dinner."

"That's okay."

She felt him reaching for something. "You're right," he said.

Ava turned to him when he didn't leave. She saw him reading one of the mangas she'd left beside the bed.

"I can see why Jackson likes it," he said. "You could cosplay this any day." He pointed to a sexy image of a warrior princess.

Ava smiled at the thought of him wanting her to dress up as one of the characters. "Be careful what you wish for."

James squeezed his eyes shut and moved his lips without saying anything.

"What are you doing?"

He opened one eye. "Wishing very hard."

She playfully slapped him. "I told you I'm ready to go to sleep."

"Go ahead. I won't bother you."

She stared at him confused. "You can't stay here."

"Why not?"

She blinked, dumbfounded. "Because I don't—"

"Relax, I just want to look at a couple more pages."

"You can take the book with you."

"I know. I don't want to. I'm comfortable where I am."

Ava hesitated. He couldn't stay. She'd never spent the night with a man. She hadn't had many relationships, but when she did the guy was usually gone the moment they finished, having James linger felt strange, even more intimate than what they'd just done. His room was only down the hall; he had no reason to stay. Why was he still there? The manga was interesting, but not enough. It didn't make sense to her.

He set the book aside. "I thought you said you wanted to sleep."

"You're leaving now?"

He lay down beside her and drew her close, holding her snuggly. "Let's try this for a minute, if you don't fall asleep in five minutes I'll leave."

That sounded reasonable. She wouldn't sleep. She'd count every second. She didn't cuddle. It was unnecessary. She licked her lip. She wished her heart didn't feel as if it were going a hundred kilometers an hour, but once he was gone it would return back to normal.

Normal. Why did his arms around her feel so normal, ordinary, and right? She felt as if she was right where she belonged. But that was wrong. He was one of them. The dreaded Fortunes. She wouldn't close her eyes, she wouldn't lean back against him, she wouldn't fall asleep…

Chapter Twenty-seven

"James and Ava are late," Edgar said with irritation as he, Rudy and Flo sat at the dinner table. Jackson had gone home.

"We can start dinner without them," Flo said, a private smile touching her lips as she filled her plate.

Edgar looked at her wondering what her secret expression meant. Her smile was always a mystery to him. It was one of the first things that had intrigued him even though he'd sought her out for very different reasons.

"I could help you win more favors and funds if you changed your image," his business mentor had told him as they stood together in the formal living room of a mutual friend. The cocktail party was lively and filled with influential people, but Edgar wished he were elsewhere.

"What do you have in mind?" he'd asked, feigning interest.

"Not what, but who."

The 'who' had captured his interest and moments later he was introduced to Flo who smiled prettily at him with that same secretive smile. He still wondered what she'd thought of him that first meeting. He knew he'd been less than gracious, giving her little opportunity to reject his advances, confident in his ability to impress her.

His friend had been right. Flo and her three boys had given his image the boost he needed, especially Rudy. That had garnered him extra bonus points. Rudy was the only one of his stepsons who called him Dad, but it was expected since Edgar was the only father he'd ever known. He made sure that their biological father didn't reappear, now that his sons were provided for (persuading him with a handsome financial incentive and soft threats). It had taken three months to convince Flo to marry him. He'd anticipated token resistance, he knew women liked not to appear overeager, but she'd made a surprisingly easy, conquest agreeing the moment he'd shown her the ring.

And now she was dying.

Fortunately, the boys were grown. It would have been more of a hassle if they'd been younger. He'd adopted them after all and they would have been his responsibility, but a good boarding school would have taken care of that problem.

He told himself that at least they'd had good years together, he'd given her a good life. But the guilt still remained.

He needed a cigar.

After dinner he went to the back patio, grabbing his coat from the closet. Although the sun still lingered in the sky the evening was cool. He no longer smoked inside the house because of Flo's illness. He stepped outside and put on the coat a faint scent drafting around him. The smell of

Lynn's perfume. He wished she wouldn't wear such a strong scent, he'd warn her next time. He lit his cigar and took a puff.

He didn't want anyone getting suspicious. Now wasn't the time for anyone to know what he was up to. It would ruin his image, one he'd taken years to build. He couldn't let a woman destroy it. He couldn't let his true weakness be discovered.

Chapter Twenty-eight

Ava woke up with a start. She opened her eyes and saw the room cloaked in darkness. She'd fallen asleep. She sighed and squeezed her pillow then paused when she realized the warm, solid form wasn't her pillow at all. She had her head on James's chest, her arm draped across him. She quickly sat up.

"What is it?" he mumbled.

Her face burned. She'd never done something like this before. To have him stay was one thing (Why was he still here?), to even let her hold him was another (How could she have let herself fall asleep in his arms?), but for her to cling to him? That was completely foreign. For a moment she didn't know herself. What if he'd wanted to leave and she'd forced him to stay because he hadn't wanted to wake her? She turned on the side light. "You should have pushed me away."

James squinted against the glare and stretched his arms above his head. "Why would I want to do that?" A slow smile spread on his face. "I know you like me." He pointed at her with mock severity. "Don't try to deny it."

She grabbed his finger. "I liked what we did. It's nothing personal. Don't get confused."

He pulled her down and locked her in his arms. "It's personal all right." His voice deepened into huskiness. "Very personal."

Ava didn't move. There was no point in lying. Would he taunt her? Tell her that he'd warned her not to fall for him?

"How would you like to get away for the weekend?"

"Alone? With me?"

"Of course with you," he said with a laugh. "Who else?"

She bit her lip. "What are we doing James?" she asked, knowing their relationship had changed.

"If you say 'yes' I'll show you."

She never imagined that saying "yes" would lead her to the Caribbean.

James flew her to Grenada, a small island that lulled Ava into a tropical embrace where for three days she thought she'd touched paradise. They spent every night in each other's arms. During the day, they snorkeled in the clear blue waters and sailed against a cloudless sky, took a tour along one of the waterfalls, inhaling the fragrant scent of nutmeg trees.

Ava indulged in the rainfall shower and luxurious soaker tub of their cottage, and lounged on the private patio where they had every meal delivered—Breakfast (fried bake and saltfish), lunch (callaloo soup), afternoon tea and dinner (chicken stew and pumpkin mash). They wandered in the market where farmers sold fresh fruit and spices and walked hand-in-hand along the boutique lined roads of the French-colonial capital of St. George's where James bought her a multicolored, spaghetti strap dress, wedges and an off-the-shoulders floral blouse to wear over jeans.

At a small village they stopped to listen to the sound of steel drums and joined the festivities of a weekly fish fry. For a sweet treat, James bought her Grenadian ginger fudge and coconut drops.

"I know the owners of the resort," James said on their last day on the island. They walked barefoot along the white sand beach mere steps from the patio of their private cottage and marveled at the natural beauty around them, "They pay careful attention to the environment, recycling plastic bottles to a local medical clinic, using produce from local farms, even using hot water solar heating and more. I like to patronize businesses like this." He turned to her. "In case you were wondering why I didn't choose a hotel."

Ava looped her arm through his; surprised he'd think she could be disappointed. "I love it here. This has been a wonderful holiday."

"I guess we'll have to come again."

Her heart skipped a beat. Another time. Would there be another time for them? She sighed, saying what was truly in her heart for the first time, "I'd like that."

Chapter Twenty-nine

"Someone is looking extra pretty today," Flo said one morning when she found Ava in the kitchen with James as they finished strawberry covered pancakes and scrambled eggs before they headed for work.

Ava blushed.

"Leave it, Mom," James said.

"At least you're finally acting like the newlyweds I expected you to be," Flo said without apology. "And when I'm gone, don't forget how easily it is to put your work before each other."

He sighed. "I hate when you talk like that. You haven't gone anywhere yet."

"But I will," she said with a resigned smile.

"We'll remember," Ava said before James could argue, sensing how much the conversation hurt him.

She sat down in front of them. "And don't forget me either."

James put down his fork, his patience thinning. "Cut it out."

"I'm trying to let you know that you don't have to worry about me anymore."

James lifted his fork and continued eating. Flo looked at him, sadness in her eyes. Ava realized his mother didn't know that James found her words painful rather than comforting.

"I'm going to go to work late, today," Ava said. "I'd love to spend some time with you in the garden."

Flo's eyes brightened. "Really? Aren't you busy?"

"No," Ava said pleased she'd eased some of the tension between mother and son. "I can make the time."

Later that evening, Ava saw James sitting in the great room reading another manga. He had his back to her so she walked up behind him, wrapped her arms around his neck and planted a quick kiss on his cheek.

"I know your mother's words bothered you this morning, darling, but she really wants you to know that she's okay." She pressed another kiss against his neck, then touched a location where last night she'd made a faint scar. "You must be a fast healer," she said surprised. "I'm afraid I was extra rough last night, but you know that about me." She touched the smooth surface again. "But it almost looks like it was never there."

Never there.

Something clicked in her mind and her heart turned cold when she looked down and saw that James's trousers weren't his usual grey but rather a deep purple. She hadn't kissed James, she'd kissed Jackson!

He turned to her and flashed a knowing smile.

"The witch has a heart," Jackson said with a cruel laugh.

Ava took a step back, horrified. She should have been more careful.

"You're in love with him."

"No, I'm not."

"Put your arms around me again, maybe I was mistaken, *darling*."

Ava gripped her trembling hands behind her back, it was her fault for laying her heart bare for him to stomp on and mock. She'd never called anyone 'darling' before. Nobody had ever been as dear to her as James, and now she was having that fact thrown back in her face. She deserved it. She'd forgotten her place and why she was there. From the triumphant look in Jackson's eyes, he knew he could hurt her if he wanted to.

He clicked his tongue in pity and stood. "Don't worry. I won't say anything." He patted her on the shoulder. "I'll save you the humiliation."

Ava pulled out her cell phone and showed him a picture of her with a smiling Flo. "I make her happy."

"I know. That's the only reason why you're still here." He left the room, leaving the manga behind.

Ava sunk down into the seat, staring at the illustrated cover that soon grew blurry as tears built behind her eyes. She buried her face in her hands.

She soon felt arms around her. "Ava, what's wrong?"

She knew that voice, that touch. He'd grown too precious to her. How could she have been so foolish as to fall in love with him?

She let her hands fall and met his kind gaze before she caught a glimpse of Jackson's smug smile as he passed in the hallway. *I'll save you the humiliation.* She had to remember that none of this was real. James would enjoy her as long as she kept his mother happy. Once that was over…plus she had to remember Edgar. Edgar was why she was here. She wiped away her tears and smiled. "How embarrassing." She lifted up the manga. "A favorite character died," she lied, feeling as if some part of her had died too.

Chapter Thirty

Pain.

Ava sat cross the dark booth in the cheap, mostly empty restaurant her father had found so that they could speak without being seen.

Although Ava knew her father loved her, she always associated him with pain. Pain from regret, betrayal, misery. He'd had a hard life. She knew it was her fault that his marriage had dissolved. Her mother and him had great plans for her, believing her to be brilliant until the year she turned three and failed the entrance exam to a prestigious pre-school. That's when they realized she was just ordinary.

Her mother couldn't bare her disappointment and left, a sting Ava still felt. She worked hard trying to prove herself, wanting to be great enough so that her mother would come back one day and say, "I was wrong", but that day hadn't arrived yet.

Because of her mother's desertion, her father never re-married, although at times Ava dreamed of him doing so or finding a woman with children of her own so that she could have siblings to play with. Instead, it was always just the two of them living in a cold dark apartment wherever he managed to get an appointment because of his erratic behavior from one university to another, before having to move on.

Every moment he could he told her about the Fortunes—how they were the reason she was without spending money, how they were the reason she'd have to work after school, how they were the reason his life, and thus hers, was one of struggle. Growing up she'd envied the Fortune's familial bond based on the stories her father managed to share about them, plus the online clippings she read of their various accomplishments and over the years her desire for revenge grew.

After the mistake with Jackson, Ava was more cautious and was eager to finally put her father's plan into action; she'd been preparing for the role for years. (She knew she didn't have much time.) Before meeting Jackson she'd spent hours learning as much as she could about him—what he liked, didn't like—and used it to seduce him. His betrayal by switching places with his brother was very clever; but marrying James as a countermeasure had proven to be more of a problem than a solution. Yes, she was now a member of the Fortune family, but she hadn't planned on her feelings.

Her heart would give her no relief. As much as she wanted to continue to despise James, fueled by years of hate, he seemed to dilute her resolve every day with a word, a touch or a look. And the nights she'd spent with him had proven to be dangerous.

For the first time, when he took her to Grenada, she felt guilty. She'd never felt that way before, not with Jackson and she knew she owed the Fortunes nothing. They owed her.

But as she spent time with Flo and Rudy she kept wondering where the monsters were. Where were the beasts her father had described all these years?

Ava picked up the paper menu that was missing a corner and was stained with ketchup. "Let's order something."

Her father snatched the menu from her, motioned to a waiter, and said, "Two coffees," before handing the menus to the young man with tiny hooped earrings. "I didn't come here to eat," Walter said. There was no anger in his voice, but it was reflected in his angular, handsome face. He had skin the color of caramel, but there was nothing sweet about him.

"I just thought—"

"It's been nearly two months."

"I'm still—"

"You haven't spoken to Lortis yet," her father said.

"I will."

He shook his head. "That's not what I want to hear."

"I'm still settling in."

"You've had more than enough time."

"Rudy was sick and I was worried about Flo—" The feel of her father's hand against her cheek stopped her words. Ava stared at him stunned. He'd never hit her before. He'd pinch her as a child, until he brought tears to her eyes; he'd sometimes kick her in the ankles when he felt she was talking back or not paying attention, but he'd never slapped her.

His eyes burned. "Have you forgotten who you belong to? You may have married a Fortune, but you're a Hughes. Is that clear?"

"Yes."

"You will fly to New York within two days."

"I can take the train."

"You will fly and secure the shares we need. Understood?"

"Yes."

"And if I see you grow soft like that again, I will finish this myself."

She nodded.

He softened his tone and reached out and touched her hand. "You're all I have. I can't let them take you away from me too. I'm sorry." He tenderly touched her cheek. "I'm sorry. I shouldn't have lost my temper."

"It's okay. I won't disappoint you." It was her fault. Her father provided for her and was good to her. She'd let him down, just as she had years ago as a child. James would forget her, but her father was all she had. The only person who truly loved her.

Chapter Thirty-one

"What happened to your face?"

Ava jumped when she entered the foyer and saw James. He wasn't supposed to be home yet and her dark skin hid bruises well. Only a sharp eye would notice. How could he see it so quickly? She lightly touched her cheek. Was there swelling?

"What are you doing home?"

He folded his arms. "What happened?"

She thought of telling him that she'd been clumsy but knew he'd see through such a lie. She had to make him angry instead. "I told you I liked it rough and I found someone who liked it too."

His eyes darkened with an emotion she couldn't read—she wanted anger but what she saw looked like something too close to hurt and disappointment. She inwardly grimaced hoping it was the former. If he hated her, that would make her job easier.

He nodded then walked away.

Ava let out a breath and headed towards the stairs.

James grabbed her wrist and spun her to him, his eyes blazing. "I will let you get away with that once, but while you're married to me you stay exclusive. Understood?"

She welcomed the hard grip of his hand, the rage in his eyes. *Yes, hate me James. Hate me for your own good.* She blinked, pretending to look bored. "Understood."

"Do you think I'm kidding?"

"No."

"I think you do." He lifted his hand to strike her then stopped and swore. "You lied."

Her heartbeat throbbed in her ears. "What?"

He wrapped his arms around her and held her close. "I'm sorry," he said with feeling. "I had to see for myself."

Mixed feeling surged through her. What was he doing? Why was he holding her like this? Why did she want him to? Why did she want to bury her face in his neck and cry? She steeled herself against the desire and kept her voice steady. "What are you talking about?"

He drew away and met her gaze. "You're not used to being hit in the face. I just saw fear in your eyes."

She pushed him away, feeling exposed and vulnerable. "I said I won't be with anyone else again. At least until we end this charade."

"Who did this to you?"

Ava turned away. "I have lovers. There's no need to be jealous."

James grabbed her chin and searched her eyes. "There's that look again. That fear. What are you hiding?"

She struggled to release herself. "Let go. You're hurting me."

He tightened his grip. "Why? I thought this is what you liked."

She tried to spin away; he pulled her back against him, but his grip didn't hurt. He trapped her with casual restraint, but not pain, and that hurt more. She wanted to free herself from his tender embrace.

"Tell me who hurt you," he whispered, his voice warm against her ear.

She blinked back tears. *Don't pretend to care about me, I can't bear it.*

"Ava? What are you afraid of?"

She searched her mind for another lie. "I told an old lover I didn't want to see him again. He didn't take it well and that's all you need to know."

James fell silent for a moment then said, "Why did you lie to me?"

"Because…I was embarrassed."

"Will he bother you again?"

"No."

He kissed her behind the ear. "Tell me his name."

"No."

"Please."

The childishly insistent tone of his voice made her reluctantly smile. "No."

He released her. "Okay."

She bit her lip then turned to him. "I have to go on a business trip, but I'll be back in a day or two."

"Okay." He gently touched her bruised cheek. "Could you give me his initials?"

She playfully pushed his hand away. "I'm a big girl. I can take care of myself."

"I know that." His smile fell. "But I'm a big boy who doesn't like his things being touched."

"I'm a thing?"

"You're my woman."

"In name only."

James shook his head. "No, I didn't say my wife. I said my woman."

"There's a difference?"

He looked at her for a long moment then he kissed her on the forehead. "Have a safe trip."

Chapter Thirty-two

Someone had hit her and she'd lied to him. He didn't know which bothered him more.

James walked into the library and sat with a book he'd pulled from the shelves, but couldn't settle his mind to read. He closed the book and set it aside.

"What's on your mind?" Jackson asked, picking up the book. He read the complicated scientific title and frowned, "Are you trying to put yourself to sleep?"

James took the book from him and replaced it on the shelf, annoyed. His brother had never stopped by the house as many times as he had over the past couple of months, but James suspected the reason. "Ava's hiding something," he said.

Jackson's brows shot up. "You're only figuring that out now? She's a conniving, manipulative—"

James pinned him with a look. "What are you hiding?"

"Nothing."

"I get this feeling that you two know something I don't."

Jackson shrugged.

"Is she in trouble?"

"No."

"Are you?"

"We all are, but I don't have proof so don't ask me any more questions. Just be careful. Don't fall for her."

"Why not?"

"That's a joke, right? She told me…" He stopped and shook his head.

"What?"

"Forget about making her fall for you. She told me how much she feels trapped having to pretend for Mom."

James's brows rose in amazement. "She said that?"

He nodded.

James accepted the stinging truth of his brother's words. No matter how much he cared about her, being with him and part of his family wasn't what she'd bargained for. Was that why she'd lied to him? She wanted to be free, but he didn't want to let her go.

Jackson watched his brother take another book from the shelf, feeling a twinge of guilt. He'd never seen a lie have such an impact. He hadn't meant to hurt his brother, but knew James was becoming too attached to Ava. He hadn't realized how much until that moment.

Jackson glanced at a light fixture, making a personal note to remind Abigail to have it dusted, then stole a look at James again. He told himself he was lying for James's sake. That it was the only way to keep him safe. He'd rather hurt his brother than let Ava get the chance to.

Success!

Ava returned from her trip to New York brimming with joy. She stepped out of the car and stared up at the Virginia mansion, seeing it in a new light. It wasn't her home, it was just another step to her true destiny. One day her father could afford a place like this and he'd be happy again.

She had a lot to tell her father and was eager to find her way back into his good graces. He hadn't spoken to her since they'd seen each other at the restaurant, now she had a reason to make him proud.

The trip had given her the distance she needed to see everything with clarity. She'd gotten too close to the Fortunes and that had clouded her view. Especially, James. She'd become a little too complacent. Now she was back on track. Victory was in sight.

Abigail met her at the door with a somber expression. "I hope your journey was good?" she asked, taking her bags.

"It was great, thank you."

Abigail began to turn then James stopped her. "I'll take these." When she hesitated, he said, "It's okay."

She nodded then left them alone.

Ava opened her mouth to offer him a greeting, but he looked away and set her bags in the corner. "There's no need to unpack."

She put up her guard, sensing something was wrong. Had he found out something? Had they discovered the true reason for her trip to New York? Had someone leaked about her meeting with Lortis? "Why? I don't understand."

James rested his hands on his hips. "We don't have to pretend anymore." His gaze lowered as did his voice. "Mom died yesterday."

Chapter Thirty-three

"But that's impossible," Ava said, refusing to believe what she'd heard. "She was fine a couple of days ago. I was just with her in the garden."

"Ava—"

"I even called her from New York and she sounded great. Full of life. We laughed about—" Her throat tightened and she fought against tears. "You said six months. It's barely been three, how could this have happened?"

"It was an infection. It caught us all off-guard. We thought it was a minor cough, but it quickly progressed to something else and spread faster than anyone expected. She passed peacefully. Just tell me where you want me to send your things."

She hesitated not understanding his cold words and behavior. They'd parted as lovers and now he was treating her like a stranger. "But I don't have to leave yet."

"It's up to you." His cell phone rang. "Excuse me," he said before he turned and walked away.

Ava stood frozen in the foyer, not knowing what to do, where to go or what to think. Flo wasn't supposed to be dead. She'd even bought her a gift, a silly little T-shirt with a picture of Lady Liberty holding a garden cushion and hoe.

She was supposed to have more time. How could Flo be gone? Why did she feel so bereft? Wasn't this what she wanted? Now she could focus on her main goal. Ava grabbed her bags without thinking, needing something to do, and headed to her bedroom.

She hesitated when she walked past Rudy's bedroom and saw him sitting on the bed staring down at his hands.

"Are you okay?" she asked him.

He looked up and shook his head.

"I'm sorry about your mom."

He pursed his lips. "I'm angry at her."

Ava set her bags down in the hallway, entered the room and sat down beside him. "Why?"

His voice cracked and tears filled his eyes. "She left without telling me she was going to heaven. I don't know why she didn't tell me first."

Ava hugged him, hoping to offer him comfort. "It happened so fast she didn't know."

An hour later, after sitting alone in her room, trying to decide her next move, Ava returned downstairs and found James sitting alone in the great room. She took the time to make sure it was really him, scanning his clothes and the way he sat just to make sure. But although she knew it was

James she felt as if a chasm had suddenly formed between them and she didn't know when or how.

But his pain was palpable.

Maybe that was it. This loss changed everything and she felt helpless.

She'd slept with him, but didn't know how to comfort him. She'd never comforted someone before.

"After the funeral we can announce our separation," James said without turning.

She started; surprised he knew she was there. She entered the room and sat in front of him. "Let's not discuss that right now. How are you? What do you need?"

"Nothing."

"Anything you want?"

He closed his eyes and a smile spread across his face. "Peaches."

Ava frowned. "I was being serious."

He looked at her. "Me too. My mom used to take me to the farmers' market to buy them when they were in season. She'd show me how to choose them, and I remember how she looked when she smelled them." His smile fell and for a moment he looked like a little boy who'd lost his mother and that tore at her heart.

"I've never selected peaches before," Ava said, not knowing what else to say. Desperate to ease the pain in his eyes.

"Really?"

"Most of my fruit comes out of the can."

James glanced at his watch. "Then let's go now. The market's still open." He stood. "I don't want to leave Rudy alone right now. Do you mind if he joins us?"

"No, of course not. I'll get him."

Ava enjoyed the unfamiliar sights and sound of the farmers' market under the warmth of the summer sun. For the new adventure, she wore the floral print blouse James had bought her in Grenada. When he saw her, his gaze lit with appreciation for a brief moment then disappeared to something more distant, confusing her.

At the market she listened patiently while both Rudy and James showed her how to pick different fruits. Back at home, they made a peach crumble, scenting the kitchen with the smell of sweet peaches, cinnamon, and brown sugar. James teased Ava about using the metric system to measure the ingredients. They served the dessert with vanilla ice cream, sat together and laughed while remembering   Flo.

"I wish she were here now," Rudy said, scooping up a large portion of his dessert. "She'd like this." He sniffed. "I miss her."

James patted him on the back. "It's okay to be sad. I miss her too."

"Are you sure she's not coming back?"

James nodded. "I'm sure."

He picked up his bowl and stood. "I'd done. Thanks Ava." He kissed her on the cheek. "I love you."

She smiled. "I love you too."

James watched his brother leave the kitchen then sat back in his chair. "Thanks for today. I needed that."

"I did too. I learned a lot."

He carried his plate over to the sink. "I'd like to stay friends."

"I'd like to stay married."

He spun around and stared at her in surprise. "But you told Jackson that—" He stopped and turned on the faucet.

Ava walked over to him. "I told Jackson what?"

He shook his head. "Doesn't matter now." He rubbed the back of his neck. "You want to see this through?"

"At least for another three months."

"Why?"

I don't know. I don't know what I'm doing! "Because it doesn't feel right to end things yet."

James looked at her for a long moment then nodded. "Rudy?"

"Yes, but–"

"You're worried about how the stockholders will feel about a funeral and divorce so close together."

"No, that's not—"

"It makes sense. You're thinking more clearly than I am. Edgar would be proud."

She sighed. She'd gotten what she wanted, more time with him, but it felt like a hollow victory.

Chapter Thirty-four

"This is the perfect time to strike," Walter told her over the phone once she'd shared the news about Flo.

Ava sat in her car staring up at the BioMed Solutions headquarters standing tall against the cloudy blue sky. "I just don't think—"

"Are you getting soft on me? Have you forgotten what they have stolen from me? Stolen from us? This is your chance. They are weak and it will make it easy for you."

She sighed. To hurt them at such a painful time may have seemed smart three months ago, but now it felt cruel. She couldn't hurt James this way. But Edgar? Edgar was another target entirely. And she kept waiting for Jackson to strike, but he hadn't yet. When he'd arrived for dinner the evening of the funeral, she'd managed to get a moment alone with him on the patio.

"Don't say anything to James yet."

Jackson leaned against the railing. "Why not? Mom's gone so you can't hurt her."

"James has already gone through enough."

Jackson sent her a cold look. "When did you start caring about him? About any of us?"

"I liked your mother."

"Sure. That's why you were sleeping with her son and conning her husband right under her nose and with her blessing. I stayed quiet but I'm not going to anymore."

"What do you want?"

His eyes pierced hers. "You. Out. Of. Our. Lives. Especially my brother's. You've been able to toy with him long enough."

She felt frantic. She didn't want to lose James; she didn't want him to know the truth. Not yet. "I'm not toying. I really—"

"Love him?" Jackson finished. "That's your problem not mine."

"I will be out of your lives in—"

"Tonight. That's all the time you have," he said then left her alone on the patio.

She had to do something before he did. Perhaps she could please her father and protect James by revealing who the true traitor was.

Dinner that evening was somber, even though Jackson had joined them and tried to make Rudy laugh, Flo's absence felt like a heavy weight around the room. Ava thought of her as she gathered the courage to do what she needed to do. She turned to Edgar. "I didn't want to say this, but I saw you with another woman. Now that Flo's gone are you ready to tell us her name?"

Edgar didn't look up from his plate of rice and stir-fried vegetables. He continued to eat as if she hadn't spoken.

"Or are you going to keep her in the shadows a little while longer for the sake of appearance?"

He wiped his mouth with a napkin. "Rudy, go to your room. You can finish your dinner there."

"But Dad—"

"Now."

Rudy shuffled away.

"He'll find out eventually," Ava said. "You can't shield him from the truth forever."

"What are you talking about?" James asked.

"I was hoping your stepfather would tell you," Ava said, staring at Edgar's calm expression. "Since Flo is gone it doesn't matter anymore."

James turned to him. "What is she—"

Edgar shook his head. "I don't know."

"I saw you with her," Ava said.

"You were seeing another woman?" James said.

"No."

"Yes," Ava countered. "An attractive younger woman." She sniffed. "I'm not surprised to hear you deny it."

"There was nobody else," Edgar said firmly.

Ava took out her cell phone and held out the picture she'd taken of them. "You call this nobody?"

Edgar's jaw twitched. "You were spying on me?"

"I saw you both by accident. I shouldn't have seen it at all. I knew you could be heartless but to cheat on your dying wife—"

Edgar grabbed her phone, slammed it on the ground and crushed it under his heel. "The matter is closed."

"Who is that woman?" James asked.

Ava reached to pick up her broken phone, but Edgar kicked it away. "I was never with another woman."

James nodded. "I believe you, Dad."

It was the first time James had ever called him that. Edgar didn't know if it was a slip of the tongue or a strategic move, but it affected him. He hung his head in shame and despair. "Her name was…is Lynn. She is a healing psychic. She promised me that she could heal your mother. That she'd done it for many others before. There was proof. I met some of her clients. Your mother wouldn't see her, but Lynn said that she didn't need to touch whoever she helped."

James shook his head. "But—"

"I know it sounds strange, but people pray for loved ones faraway, don't they? Is it wrong to want help?"

"How much did you pay her?"

"I'm not proud of what I did. I know what investors would think if they knew the truth. That's why I kept it a secret. I didn't use any company funds. No money can be traced to her."

"How much?"

"For a while it seemed to be working. You saw it too, didn't you? Your mother had more energy and seemed so happy. And the pain wasn't what it had been."

"Just give me a range," James said.

"It doesn't matter. I would have paid her millions if it would give your mother one more day." He turned to Ava with cold eyes. "I loved my wife. So much so I didn't tell her the truth about you. I made sure not to let her know what you've been up to behind our backs."

Ava felt her skin grow cold. How could she have been wrong about him? Everyone knew the marriage had been one of convenience. Edgar Fortune didn't love anything but money, right? He was lying. There was no psychic healer and what could he possibly know about her? He was trying to shift blame and confuse her. "I was only thinking about Flo when I saw you with that other woman. I didn't mean to—"

"You can stop the act. I know you've been trying to buy up shares. I had a very informative conversation with Lortis who likes to keep me up-to-date about things. Your pathetic little purchases won't do much harm. I don't know the reason, but whatever you're planning won't work."

Ava kept her voice level. "I'm not planning anything."

Edgar rested his elbows on the table and clasped his hands together. "In boxing there are many great moves. The Haymaker, The Bolo Punch. I really like the Jab and Grab, which is a mixture of offense and defense. You lead in with a jab and quickly proceed to grab your opponent. It helps to neutralize any more attacks coming at you." He leaned forward. "But my favorite is The Body Drop Feint. It's a move of distraction. It allows your opponent to think you are about to do one thing, like punch him in a certain way, while you switch it up with another punch aimed at a different spot. You really should have thought carefully before trying to tussle with me."

"I know—"

"I taught my boys the same. James was a master at distraction. I'm sure you've seen some of his moves, but not all of them. Do you really know who you're in love with?"

"Not now," James said in a warning voice.

"Do you think he needs your protection?" Edgar continued. "He's the strongest of all of us. I thought I was tough, until I met this kid. This kid knows where his allegiance should be. You will not come between us."

Jackson flashed a cruel smile. "Did you really think you were part of this family? Did you really think you were the only one pretending for Mom's sake? She was the only reason you lasted as long as you did. James is a master player and he played you. You think that trip to Grenada happened by accident?" Jackson tapped his chest. "I helped him choose the spot."

"That's enough," James said.

"He wanted to make Mom happy, but with her out of the picture, there's no longer a reason for you to stay."

Ava didn't dare look at James, afraid to see what would shine in his eyes. Had it all been a lie? Grenada was just a plan to seduce her? She remembered his first warning, *When I seduce a woman she doesn't know it.* She now saw all his care and tenderness as an act.

"Ava," James said. "That's not—"

"You don't have to console her," Jackson said, "or worry about getting a divorce. You married an imposter."

James turned to his brother. "What?"

Jackson nodded. "Your marriage isn't legal because she married you under a false name. Her real name is—"

"What are you talking about?" Ava said. "Ava is my real name."

"Sure it is. And you haven't been buying up stock either, right?"

"I admit to that. My father is Walter Hughes and he once worked with your stepfather in the early days. But Edgar stole his ideas and took everything from him, forcing my father to flee the country and start over again. I just wanted my father to have a taste of the revenge he deserved."

"What's her real name?" Edgar asked Jackson. "I want to understand what's going on."

"Amelia Bremmer."

"And her father?"

"Walter Bremmer."

Edgar nodded then turned to Ava with pity. "Your

father lied to you."

"My father would never—"

"He did work briefly with me as did your mother. She was a talented office manager and I respected her. When she asked for my help I agreed. I know that doesn't fit my reputation, but it's the truth. Your father, at the time, made your mother very unhappy."

"My father was a brilliant man. He gave you ideas. I saw his notes."

"Maybe, but he didn't share them with me. There was no exchange of ideas. He had nothing to do with the founding of BioMed Solutions. He'd briefly worked in one of the labs that was all. Whatever he's told you is from his imagination. The last time I saw your father it was in a courtroom. Your mother had divorced him and wanted to get custody of you. My testimony helped her win that case and your father never forgave her. Or me. He kidnapped you and disappeared."

"No." Ava swallowed hard, bewildered by his words. "My mother left me. She—"

"She's been looking for you, for years."

Ava jumped to her feet. "This is all a lie. My father would never hurt me like this."

James rose too and took her arm. "Go upstairs. I'll be there in a minute."

She yanked her arm away. "Don't pretend to care," she said before she stormed out of the room.

Chapter Thirty-five

J ackson stared at his brother outraged. "You're letting her stay here? You should have kicked her out immediately."

James sat down and glared at him. "Keep your voice down."

"Why? She's dangerous. Didn't you hear what I just said?"

He looked at Jackson then Edgar. "I know, but we must also think about Rudy. He's gone through a lot and is already struggling with depression. More change could—"

"Don't you care what she's done?"

"Of course I care."

"Maybe not enough," Edgar said. "You let her get to you."

James turned away. "That's not it."

"She forced you to marry her," Jackson said.

"I know that."

"By having me locked up in a room with two thugs and telling me that I had to disappear for two days." Jackson nodded at his brother's look of surprise. "Yes, that's the secret she wanted me to keep hidden from you. She was no innocent in this mess. I would have played my role and arrived at the reception as we'd agreed if she hadn't interrupted our plans."

"What plans?" Edgar said.

"It's a long story," James said. He looked at Jackson. "I still think you went too far. You shouldn't have mentioned Grenada."

Jackson's brows shot up. "Are you feeling sorry for that thing? That creature from the Black Lagoon?"

"That's enough."

"One of her thugs even punched me."

"I'm not saying what she did was right, but she's a victim in all this too. Her father stole her from her mother and has been lying to her for years."

Edgar shook his head. "She won't believe anything you say. Walter Bremmer was a master manipulator. That's how he first tricked her mother into marrying him before showing his true colors. He even charmed the judge, but I was able to break through his façade." He fixed James with a look. "I'll tell you this only once. She doesn't deserve you. Getting her out of our lives will be the best thing for everyone. I want her out by tomorrow."

James sighed resigned, then went to Ava's room not surprised to see she was already gone. She'd left her ring behind on the pillow.

Chapter Thirty-six

Edgar retreated to his bedroom surprised by what he'd just heard. He sat on his bed and shook his head. Walter Bremmer had resurfaced in his life. Flo would have been shocked. He wished she was there to see how everything had unraveled. How the quiet little girl they'd briefly seen, had grown up. He hadn't wanted to get involved initially, but when he told Flo about his office manager's request to help her get custody of her only child, she was the one who'd urged him to testify in court against Walter. She had such a good heart.

He grabbed her pillow, held it close and cried. He fought not to make a sound as the depths of his sorrow bubbled out. His joy and peace. His life. He'd married her for gain and lost his heart instead.

He remembered kneeling by her bedside one last time. The light touch of her hand on his face, her weak smile. With all his money he couldn't make her well.

"Don't look at me like that," she said.

"There's something you should know," he said, ready to reveal the truth that had been a guilty thorn in his heart.

"I know Rudy was the real reason you married me. I know you wanted a child with special needs to improve your image and make you appear as someone you weren't. I know you also chose my sons so that you could have them look up to you, depend on you and serve you. I know I was the last part of your plan, a wife that would an accessory to your ambition." She took his hand. "I knew all that and I fell in love with you anyway. What does that say about me?"

He took her hand, pressing it against his lips. "I was not a good man and this is my punishment."

"No, my darling. Think of all the years we've had together. Think of the man you've become. Take care of our boys for me."

"Always."

"And could you do something else for me? I know it will be hard but—"

"Anything."

"Say the words."

He swallowed. He'd never realized in all the years they'd been married, he'd never said the words to her. The words that had lingered in his heart since the first day he'd told her she could stay the night with him. He closed his eyes against tears. The words were hard, words he'd never said to anyone. "I love you."

He opened his eyes, childishly wishing his words would have a magical affect and make her well again.

"Thank you," she said with a tired smile, but her eyes glowed with the light of youth and joy and he knew he'd made her happy with a gift that was priceless.

Edgar remembered that gaze as he held her pillow, his tears as fresh as the pain in his heart, but he also felt gratitude. He carefully set the pillow back down, as if it were precious. He'd been able to say goodbye, to tell her how he felt. No one else had loved him like she had, it was a debt he would forever repay. And that meant keeping her boys safe, which he would do until his last breath.

Chapter Thirty-seven

Walter stared at his daughter with a bored expression. When she'd arrived at his apartment, brimming with anger, he'd expected a fight and was ready.

"What do you want?" he asked, opening the door wider.

She marched past him into the dark, cramped room and slammed the door behind her, the sound echoing down the hallway. "They told me."

"What?"

"The truth."

"What truth?"

"About Mom."

Walter sniffed. "That's one version of the story. The same story he used in court against me."

Ava stared at him. "So it is true?"

Walter hesitated, he hadn't imagined that she might have been doubting Edgar's story. Now he'd confirmed it. He slapped the wall with the flat of his hand. "I had no choice! He stripped me of my life. I wouldn't be surprised if he wasn't sleeping with her at the time."

"That's not the kind of man he is."

"You think you know him better now?" He sat down on a torn green couch the previous apartment owner had left behind. "You got used to the sweet life and you want to stay close, is that it?"

Ava quickly looked around the dingy room. "You don't have to live this way. I told you that I could help you get a better place."

"Now you're looking down on me?"

"You're lucky I'm still talking to you at all. You lied and said that Mom left."

He shrugged. "You were better off without her. She didn't realize how bright you were. You would have had a dull life with her. I wanted more for you. I gave you everything you needed."

"Except tenderness."

He winced at the word. "You didn't need that. That would have made you soft."

"I thought so too, at first until I met—"

"You were dumb enough to fall in love with him? He tossed you aside, didn't he?" He looked at her with disdain. "You should see yourself. Look at how his soft touch has made you weak. Pathetic. That's what your mother did too. Coddled you."

Ava looked at him with sadness. "You can't say it, can you?"

"Say what?"

"I'm sorry."

"Why would I say something I don't feel? You have a lot to thank me for. I hope one day you'll see it. They did steal my life. They damaged my reputation. And now they're trying to steal you away from me. Will you let them?"

"No, Dad. I'm not being taken from you because you can't lose something you've never owned."

Chapter Thirty-eight

"I don't know what to say," Camy said, her voice filled with dismay over the phone. "I always thought there might be something fishy about your father's story, but I never imagined this. He actual kidnapped you?"

Ava sat alone in her apartment on her hard couch, gripping her cell phone as if it were a life line. "Yes."

"What are you going to do?"

"I don't know where to begin. I want to find my mother, but I'm scared."

"What are you going to do about James? I know how you feel about him."

"It's over now."

Camy paused. "Give it time. Maybe—"

"There's too much to overcome. I have no one else to blame but myself. I had many chances to turn back and I didn't. You should have seen how I accused his stepfather of cheating and when Jackson tells him what I did to him after the wedding, I'm sure he'll never want to see me again."

"You know you can always come and visit. Actually I'll be entertaining another of my aunt's students. You're welcome to join us."

Ava smiled. "Thanks, but I don't think I'd be good company."

"Whenever you're ready, I'm here."

"Thanks."

Ava disconnected and hugged herself, looking around the room. Her apartment was a big improvement from the place where her father was staying, but not by much.

She'd never felt so cold. So alone. She hadn't realized how used to warmth she'd become. A warmth that had always been empty from her life, so she never missed it. She missed it now. Craved it. Wanted to fight the bone chilling ache inside her. She had no anger to fuel and warm her, leaving her hollow.

She felt as if she'd lost the only home she'd ever known. Even though it hadn't been real, it had felt real. It had felt safe. She missed James holding her, the feel of him in bed beside her, a feeling of belonging.

She began to drift off to sleep when she heard a soft knock on her front door. She looked through the peephole but the person was out of range. Was it her father? Had he come to apologize? Or was it Jackson coming to gloat?

"Who is it?"

"James."

She rubbed her hands together, trying to bank down her excitement. She couldn't jump to conclusions, she didn't know why he wanted to see her. She took a deep breath and opened the door. "Yes?"

"Can I come in?"

She hesitated then silently stepped back.

He sent a wary look at the couch then turned to her. "Why do you have a couch made up of textbooks?"

"My father and I used to move a lot and he didn't much care for furniture. But his books were his treasure so I learned to make use of them and he didn't complain. I guess I got used to it. I could get you a chair."

He shook his head and sat down. "I don't want to get too comfortable." He shook his head again, looking perplexed. "I don't know what I'm doing. I shouldn't even be here."

"Why not?"

"Because we're not going to work."

Her heart fell. She knew he couldn't forgive her. She sat down beside him, but looked straight ahead. "I see."

"Lies," he said with a tired sigh. "That's all we have between us. And now we've added my family's distrust. Do you think you can survive that? Do you want to?"

"Yes."

He turned sharply to her, amazed. "What?"

"I said yes." She licked her lower lip. "I want to be with you."

He covered his eyes. "Then I need to find a way to fix this. Any ideas?" He glanced at her when she didn't respond. "Why are you smiling?"

"You really still want to be with me?"

He nodded.

She closed her eyes and sighed with relief. She felt some warmth slipping back into her and leaned against him. "I thought I'd lost you."

"You may still lose me."

She straightened and stared at him, the cold, lost feeling returning.

"I have responsibilities," he said in a grim tone. "Do you think my brother Rudy can take any more changes? Do you think I want to live the rest of my life alienated from my brother and stepfather? It's not a choice I can make lightly."

"I understand," she said, even though it hurt.

"No, I don't think you do. I don't think you know what it's like to be ripped in two. To always try to do the right thing even though it kills you."

"I lived most of my life believing a lie. Hating the Fortunes, it felt like a betrayal falling in love with you, but I did."

His eyes narrowed suspiciously. "How do I know that this isn't part of your plan too?"

"What?"

"You wanted the Fortunes destroyed," he said in an even tone. "This could be the ultimate way to do it. I run off with you and then months from now you leave and my family is divided forever."

Ava gasped, shocked by his words. "If you think I'm capable of—"

"No," he said softly. He lightly touched her cheek. "I'm just throwing out a theory. Unfortunately, my stepfather is adamant that we can't be together."

"I could try to win him over."

James flashed a sour grin. "That would take a miracle. Once you've lost his trust, there's no way back."

"How about *your* trust?" He fell silent and his hesitation hurt her, but she fought not to let it show. "You don't have to answer that. All I ask for is some time."

"Time?"

"Wait for me," Ava said, resting her head on his shoulder, wanting to be close, even though he still felt far away. She had a renewed sense of purpose. "I'll win over your stepfather no matter what it takes." *And I'll fully win your heart too.*

Chapter Thirty-nine

She was bold. He had to give her that.

Edgar studied Ava as she sat in his office. He tapped a finger against his large oak desk, ready for a match. His assistant had announced her arrival and he'd considered ignoring her request, but then succumbed out of curiosity. It had been a week since she'd left the house.

"You have five minutes."

"I only need two. As you know I've been studying BioMed Solutions closely."

He steepled his fingers and nodded.

"And I have a proposal." She placed a report in front of him.

Edgar briefly flipped through it then stopped on one page. "You want me to cut two of my divisions?"

"I believe you can sell them off for a large profit, and then focus your company's efforts on its highest performing divisions, while also incorporating the new product my company has developed. I believe by doing so you could increase profits a hundredfold."

"I don't need you for that. We signed an agreement, you can't back out now. Your company has already been folded into BioMed Solutions. I got what I wanted for the business. And let's not forget that you have benefitted financially and will continue to do so."

"I'm still legally married to James. Ava Hughes *is* my legal name. My father completed all the correct paperwork."

"Divorcing James won't be too painful. There's still the prenup. Once you leave you get nothing." He smiled. "What's your next move?"

"Flo."

His smile disappeared. "Don't you—"

"I'm sorry. I was wrong about you and I shouldn't have accused you, especially in front of your family. But I'll admit that I'm not really here for your sake or even mine, although I do love James. I'm here because of her." She glanced at the framed picture of Flo on his desk. "She taught me so much, but one thing she showed me was that it was okay to be vulnerable. That strength comes in many forms. Her love for her family made her strong at her weakest moment. I know she taught you that too."

Edgar shook his head. "It won't work. I don't want you near my family."

"Why not? You and I are the same. We both married for selfish reasons and we both lost our hearts. The difference is…I didn't have to wait years to find out."

Edgar rose to his feet. "You should go."

Ava remained seated. "You stood up for me once. I don't know what my life would have been like if I'd been raised by my mother, but it's good to know that someone was looking out for me. If nothing else, let that little girl pay you back."

Edgar slowly sat down. "You're definitely tenacious," he said with reluctant admiration. "A knockout punch."

"What?"

He held out his hand. "You have a deal."

Chapter Forty

"What should I do with this?" Abigail asked James as he and Jackson sat watching TV in the great room. He looked up to see what she was holding in her hand and saw it was one of Ava's mangas. "I found it under the couch in the library."

"Thanks."

He reached for it, but Jackson snatched it first. "I'll make sure she gets it," he said.

Abigail nodded and walked away.

James glared at him and held out his hand. "Give it back."

"No."

"I want to return it to her myself."

Jackson returned his attention to the TV. James reached for the manga, but Jackson held him off. James grabbed him by the collar. "I'm not playing."

Jackson grabbed him by the throat. "Neither am I."

"You really want to fight me for this?"

"If I have to."

James pushed him away in disgust. "You can't stop me from seeing her."

Jackson smoothed out his collar then returned his attention to the TV.

"What are you doing here anyway?"

"Making sure she doesn't come back. I heard she visited Rudy's shop and had a meeting with Edgar."

"So what?"

"That means she's up to something."

James opened his mouth to reply, but another voice cut him off. "He's right."

The two men turned and saw Ava standing in the entryway. Before they could speak she walked up to Jackson and said, "I'm sorry. I'm sorry I had you kidnapped and held and that Camy's boyfriend punched you."

His brows shot up. "That was her boyfriend?"

"You weren't really in any danger, I just wanted you to think so. Will you ever forgive me?"

Jackson frowned, but not as fierce as he had in the past. "I don't know—"

"You might as well surrender," Edgar said, coming up behind her. He rested his hand on her shoulder. "She's not one to give up easily and you might as well get used to her. She's still part of the family." He looked at James. "Of course how *long* she stays that way depends on you."

Ava looked at him, anxious, not sure what he would say. "I know I need more time to win your trust," she said quickly, "but let's talk alone before you say anything."

James stood and sighed. "I don't want to talk." He held out his hand. "I want to be by your side when you're finally reunited with your mother."

Tears sprung to her eyes as she took his hand, happiness filling her. "Because that's what Flo would have wanted?"

"No," James said, pulling a ring from his trouser pocket. He got down on one knee and gazed up at her with his heart in his eyes. "Because I love you." He slid the ring on her finger and stood, drawing her close. "And I want to stand by your side…always."

About the Author

Dara Girard is an award-winning, national bestselling author of more than thirty books including *Sweet Temptation*, *Midnight Promise, Unexpected Pleasure,   Just One Look* and *The Amber Stone*. Dara loves to travel and hear from readers.

You can write her at:
contactdara@daragirard.com
or
P.O. Box 10345
Silver Spring, MD 20914

If you'd like to receive a reply, please send a self-addressed stamped envelope. Visit daragirard.com to join her newsletter and be the first to find out about current and upcoming releases.